ISA & THE MYSTERY

(THE SUNNYVALE MYSTERIES, BOOK 2)

JESSICA SORENSEN

Isa & the Mystery
Jessica Sorensen
All rights reserved.
Copyright © 2015 by Jessica Sorensen
This is a work of fiction. Any resemblance of characters to actual
persons, living or dead, is purely coincidental. The author holds exclusive
rights to this work. Unauthorized duplication is prohibited.
No part of this book can be reproduced in any form or by electronic or
mechanical means including information storage and retrieval systems,
without the permission in writing from author. The only exception is by
a reviewer who may quote short excerpts in a review.
Any trademarks, service marks, product names or names featured are
assumed to be the property of their respective owners, and are used only
for reference. There is no implied endorsement if we use one of these
terms.

ISBN: 9781939045690

For information: jessicasorensen.com
Cover design by MaeIDesign

❀ Created with Vellum

CHAPTER ONE

OKAY, SO I MIGHT HAVE BEEN TOO CONFIDENT AT THE hospital about how easy it was going to be to get ahold of my birth certificate. I've been searching the house for days and haven't stumbled across it yet. I did find Hannah's in a trunk in Dad and Lynn's room, so logically, mine should be in there, too. But nope. Not even my social security card was in there. I even tried looking for information on the Internet, but the only thing that came up under my name was my blog and the last entry I made on it where I broke down and rambled on about my search for my mother.

I thought about deleting the post right after I wrote it, but since I have three followers and none of them are from around here—except for Grandma Stephy—I decided it's okay to leave it up. Plus, it felt kind of good to talk about it aloud ... well, aloud in a way.

To add more complication to my life, Lynn and my dad have gone into Isabella-doesn't-exist mode. They refuse to acknowledge when I'm in the room, when I speak, or even when I "accidentally" dropped a glass cup on the floor to try to get their attention. My dad did make eye contact with me a couple of times. Mostly he just stares at me like he's seen a ghost. The look honestly creeps me out.

If it weren't for Hannah, I'd seriously believe I somehow got ahold of an invisibility cape and am unintentionally wearing it. She lets me know I still exist in the visible realm, in a very, very Hannah-like way.

"What's up with those god-awful shoes?" she asks Saturday morning as I enter the kitchen to get some breakfast.

My dad and Lynn are on vacation, so I get a break from two of the three people that hate me. If only Hannah would've gone somewhere too. Then I would've had the whole place to myself.

Sigh. A girl can dream, can't she?

I glance down at the flip-flops on my feet. "I have to wear flats because of this." I point at the bandage on my knee that covers the stitches.

"You look fucking stupid, like you're going to the beach or something, which is just dumb since we live in the mountains, and it's September. Plus, you really need a mani/pedi if you're going to wear stuff like that," Hannah sneers as she breaks apart a granola bar. Once it's in half, she reads the side of the box. "So that makes it seventy-five calories," she mutters to herself.

All the things I wish I could say to her burn at the tip of my tongue. I want to ask her if she knows about my mom, if she told anyone, if she sent me those texts while I was on my trip. But I bite them back, mostly because I'm not in the mood to war with her. And I doubt she'd just confess everything to me.

While she's calorie counting, I steal a vanilla cupcake from the platter on the kitchen island and a soda from the fridge. As I'm hurrying out of the room, her eyes zero in on me.

"Ew, is that what you're eating for breakfast?" She glares at the cupcake in my hand. "You're going to get fat if you eat like that."

"I always eat like this." I lick a huge glob of frosting off the top. "It's so yummy."

She practically drools as she eyeballs the delicious treat in my hand, and I find it oddly satisfying knowing she wants to eat the cupcake but won't.

"Good luck keeping the weight off!" she hollers after me as I dash out of the kitchen. "Oh, yeah ... and, Isa!"

"So close," I mumble to myself then lean back and pop my head into the kitchen. "Yeah?"

"Mom and Dad wanted me to tell you something." She drums her manicured nails against the granite countertop. "Hmmm ... I think it's important, but I can't remember what it is." A smirk curls at her lips. "Oh, I remember. They told me to tell you that they loved you, to be safe, and that if you need anything, to call them."

"They did?" I ask, then a second later realize my mistake.

It's too late. She's already grinning like the Cheshire Cat.

"Oh, wait," she says with a fake laugh. "That message was for me." She stands up from the barstool with half a granola bar in her hand. "They wanted me to remind you that you're not allowed to see Grandma Stephy and to make sure to clean the entire house while they're gone." She skips out of the kitchen, intentionally bumping me into the wall as she passes by.

I'm unsure if she's telling the truth or not, and I'd be lying if it didn't gut me. I hate that there's a huge chance she's not lying.

By the time I make it to my room, my eyes are watery, my chest aches with loneliness, and I've wolfed down most of the cupcake. I pop the tab on the soda and take a swig before setting it down on the nightstand. Then I stare at my plain, white walls that are patched up from all the tacks and nails I used to hold up my drawings and posters.

Indigo has yet to make it over to paint the mural, mostly because we haven't really gotten a chance. I know if my parents are around when she comes over, they'll put a stop to our painting and punish me big time. If I do paint it while they're gone, it'll take them some time to discover what I've done since they've gone back to never coming up to my room.

I decide to text Indigo so we can put the mural plan in motion while my parents are on vacation for the weekend.

Me: Hey, u wanna come over and paint my wall or what?

Indigo: Sorry! Can't today. I have a job interview.

I'm mildly bummed but super excited for her.

Me: Where?!

Indigo: At that art gallery, applying for that job I told u about.

Me: Yay! I'll keep my fingers crossed for u.

Indigo: U better. If I get this job, then I can get my own place. No offense to Grandma Stephy, but I'm getting a little tired of Friday night poker at the community center. Plus, that Harry dude has been coming over a lot. I seriously can't look either one of them in the eye when they're together.

Me: LOL! I still can't believe we walked in on them.

Indigo: I wish I could forget ... The sounds, they still haunt my nightmares.

Me: But she seems happy with this Harry dude, right?

Indigo: She really does.

Me: Good. I want her to be happy. And fingers and toes crossed u get the job!

Indigo: Thanx! Let u know when I do. Rain check on the room painting.

Me: Yep! Might go get paint supplies today, since I don't have anything else to do.

Other than look for my birth certificate. I'm honestly running out of places to look. There's only one thing I can think to do, and that's confront my dad. I'm not sure he'll even acknowledge me asking.

"When they get back from their trip, I'm going to ask my dad if I can go move in with Grandma Stephy, and then I'm going to confront him," I tell myself with fierce determination. "Right now, I'm going to go get some paint … give myself a little break from this house and this room."

I pull a face at the walls as I grab some cash from my nightstand drawer from a stash I've collected over the years. Most of it came from my grandpa. Every holiday and birthday, he gave me a card with at least ten bucks in it.

"For college," he said simply. "Or just a rainy day."

I glance out my window at the raindrops beading the glass. "Perfect. A rainy day."

I tuck a few twenties into my back pocket then stuff the rest back in the drawer and collect my jacket from my closet. I then zip up my jacket and head out in my shorts and flip-flops. I'm going to seriously freeze my butt off, but I've done the walk to town in sun, rain, and snow before and lived.

My outfit isn't that fashionable or practical for cold weather. But pulling on skinny jeans over my knee is like trying to stuff Indigo's and my movie candy stash into a purse, which never, ever worked—we both have serious sweet tooth issues.

Luckily, I hit the sister jackpot, because Hannah's nowhere in sight as I head downstairs. If she were, she'd be all over my shorts and hoodie combo.

When I reach the back door, my jackpot status goes *kerplunk* as my phone dings with another text from the unknown caller.

Unknown: I have something that could ruin your life.

Attached to the message is a photo of what looks like the corner of a piece of paper.

I have no clue what's on the piece of paper, but a cold chill runs through my body that I might soon find out.

Anger bursts through me. Dammit! I hoped this shit would stop now that I was home.

I need to find a way to get it to stop.

Before I can even think about what I'm doing, I reply.

Me: Hannah, cut this crap out. I know it's you.

I hit send, and seconds later, they respond.

Unknown: Who's Hannah?

Fear briefly flashes through me before I shake the emotion away. This is probably just another way to try to get to me. It has to be her.

I message Indigo about it, but she doesn't reply. Sighing, I then shove the phone into my pocket, wrap my fingers around the doorknob, and yank the door open.

Cold rain instantly soaks through my clothes as I limp down the driveway, moving awkwardly since I can't bend one knee. The situation should make me more upset, but I've always been a sucker for the rain. It smells so great and puts a calmness over me.

I start to skip disjointedly through the puddles, my flip-flops splashing water all over the backs of my legs. It reminds me of the time Kai and I walked home in the rain, and we intentionally splashed in all the puddles.

"Isa! What are you doing?" someone shouts with a hint of laughter in their voice.

I whip my head to the side as I stumble to a stop.

Kai is standing out on the side deck beneath the shelter of the roof. I think he's laughing at me, but the veil of rain crashing from the cloudy sky makes it difficult to see.

"Going to the paint store!" I shout back then wave before I start to skip off again.

"Are you crazy?" he calls out. "You can't walk to town in the middle of a rainstorm."

I sigh and slow down again. "I'm not walking! I'm skipping!" My eyelashes flutter against the rain.

"Can't you wait until it at least stops raining?" he asks, shaking his head as I jump into a puddle.

"No way! It's either the rain or being in the house with Hannah. And I choose the rain. Besides, rain is awesome!"

I can hear him laughing all the way from over here.

"Will you get your ass over here?" He waves at me to come to him. "I'll drive you if you really want to go. It's too damn cold for you to be playing around in the rain, no matter how cute you look."

Cute? Did he just call me cute? No, I must've heard him wrong.

I don't head over right away. Ever since the first day of school, Kai and I haven't really talked that much. He's also skipped out on a lot of classes, and the few times he has made a grand appearance, he seems exhausted and out of it. I don't want to jump to conclusions like the rest of the town, but it's almost like he wants people to think he's a troublemaker.

"Would you stop overthinking and get your ass over here?" he yells at me, smiling as he leans over the railing.

"Oh, fine. Take away my rain fun."

I hike up his driveway and dive underneath the shelter of the porch.

"That's a nice look for you. Totally weather-appropriate, too," he teases as he looks over my drenched shorts, jacket, and hair.

The black shirt, dark jeans, and studded belt he's wearing makes him look like he's trying to go Goth. It's not his normal look, so I wonder if he's going somewhere or just taking his bad boy image to a new level.

I wring my hair out. "I can't wear anything else other than shorts and sandals until my knee heals; otherwise, the stitches hurt."

"Stitches?" He frowns. "What happened?"

"I jumped out of a moving car and fell on a piece of glass." I shrug like it's no big deal.

"Very badass." He stares at me long enough to make my insecurity go up about a thousand notches. "I was actually just teasing about your clothes. Although, you definitely pull off the wet clothes look." He tugs on a wet strand and dazzles me with a lopsided smile. "Relax, Isa. I'm not making fun of you. Never have." His smile broadens. "And you look fine in wet clothes. But cold." He nods at the door. "Come on; let's get you inside."

I wrap my arms around myself as I shiver. "I am kinda freezing my ass off." My teeth clank together as the chattering sets in. "But don't worry; I'm tough."

"I know you are." He winks at me for God knows what reason. I must give him a funny look, because he laughs and says, "Relax, I don't bite," before opening the door.

We step inside the washroom where I slip off my shoes so I won't track mud all over the hardwood floors.

"You should take your jacket off, too," Kai says as he shuts the door. "My mom is weird about us tracking water through the house."

Nodding, I unzip my jacket and slip my arms out of my sleeves. Kai watches me from the doorway like I'm the most fascinating thing in the world as I hang it up on the hook near the door. Thankfully, my shirt's fairly dry, and after losing the cold, wet jacket, my body temperature starts to warm up again.

"So …" I wrap my arms around myself once more. I've never been in his house before. I feel so nervous. "You said you could take me to the store."

He nods, backing through the doorway and into the kitchen with his eyes on me. "I can give you a ride when I head out to a party if you want."

"Okay." I follow him into the kitchen, confused. "That means I'd have to walk home." I hold up my hands when he arches a brow at me. "Which is totally fine by me."

He scoops up an apple from a basket on the counter. "It'll probably be late when I head out. I'm not sure it's a good idea for you to be walking around in the rain *while* it's late."

"Um …?" Okay, I so don't get guys. Didn't he offer to take me to the store? So why does it sound like he doesn't want to now? "I guess I can just walk there right now, then."

He bites into the apple and studies me while chewing. "Or, you could just go with me."

"To a *party* with *you*?"

He chuckles, wiping juice from his chin with his sleeve. "You don't have to sound so disgusted when you say it. I promise I'm not that gross." He wavers, bobbing his head from side to side. "Now the party, on the other hand, I'm not going to make any promises."

"I don't think you're gross. I'm just confused."

"Over?"

"Over you inviting me to one of your parties. I mean, I know you said that when you were drunk, but I didn't think you were serious."

"I was—am. And it's not my party. It's Bradon's." He takes another bite of the apple. "You know, that guy you met at my locker."

"Yeah, I remember," I say, trying not to think about how he blew me off the moment Bradon showed up.

"Something's up," Kai accuses, eyeing me. "You have a tone."

I shrug, feigning dumb. "That's just how my voice sounds."

"No, it doesn't." He sinks his teeth into the apple again. "You don't like Bradon?"

"I don't even know Bradon, other than the two seconds we met at your locker."

"Then what's with the tone?"

I chew on my bottom lip and shrug.

He gives me a stern look. "Isa, don't make me get it out of you."

I roll my eyes. "You say that like you have the power to actually make me. And you don't, unless you're secretly a wizard."

He smashes his lips together, suppressing a laugh. Then, with his gaze trained on me, he sets the apple down on the counter and cracks his knuckles.

"I do know how to make you, even if I don't have magic powers. Well, unless you've become less ticklish over the last five years." He bedazzles me with an arrogant grin as I step away from him.

"You promised me when I told you my kryptonite that you'd never use it against me," I remind him as I take another step back.

He matches my move, stealing the space I put between us.

"Kai, I'm serious. You promised you wouldn't ever tickle me."

"I don't remember making such a promise."

"Oh, yeah, well …" I frantically search for a way to stop him.

"I don't know why you're acting so scared. There's nothing to get scared about. It's just a little tickling." He innocently bats his eyelashes at me

"Oh, yeah, well … FYI, you just fluttered your eyelashes like a girl." I know it's a lame attempt to get him to stop, but it's all I've got at the moment.

Of course he finds my attempt more amusing than annoying, and even laughs.

I narrow my eyes at him, trying to think of a better insult. Then I'm blindsided as he barrels toward me with his fingers ready to attack my sides.

"Kai! Stop!" I squeal, hunching over and trying to protect my sides with my arms. I snort a big, old pig laugh as he tickles the air out of me. "If you don't stop, I'm going to tell everyone at school that you know what kryptonite is and that you used to want to be Superman."

"That was in the seventh grade." He continues tickling me. "That stuff doesn't matter anymore."

I swing around him and skitter around the kitchen island, but he catches the back of my shirt.

"So, you just outgrew that phase, then, huh?" I ask between laughs as he drags me back toward him.

"No, I still think it'd be pretty cool to be Superman." He digs his fingers into my sides. His chest is pressed against my back, and his warm breath is brushing the back of my neck. "I just don't give a shit if anyone finds that out anymore."

When he stops tickling me, I peek up at him.

"You're saying that you've changed since seventh grade? That you're not that guy anymore who wants to be so popular?" I roll my eyes just to bug him.

"I'm not even close to that guy anymore," he promises, his hands still on my waist. "And it's not that crazy to change over five years. You changed over three months."

"Okay, I get your point ... I guess. It's still kind of hard to believe you've changed that much." This time, I do have a tone.

He sighs heavily. "Isa, I really am sorry I was a dick to you back then. I know it's not an excuse, but I was dealing with a lot of shit. And ..." He shrugs, which looks awkward since he still has his hands on me and his chest aligned with my back. "I've wanted to apologize to you for a while, but every time I said anything to you, you acted like I was the most annoying person in the world. And I get it. I totally deserve you treating me like that."

"You *can* be the most annoying person in the world," I tease, but my emotions get the best of me and my voice cracks. "It's okay, I guess. I mean, I get it. We were different people back then."

"It's still not okay. And I'm going to make it up to you. Somehow."

"You don't have to do that. The apology is enough." I pause. "I am a little confused about something, though. All during school last year, you teased the crap out of me. It didn't seem like you were that sorry."

"My teasing is playful," he insists, his hands sliding around to my front. "I've told you that already."

"Then why did you act like a weirdo when Bradon came up to us while we were talking at your locker?" I decide it's time to be blunt, instead of tiptoeing around everything. "It felt like you were acting weird because ... you were embarrassed to be seen with me." My chest tightens as I think about all the times people were embarrassed to be seen with me. "Which I totally get. I know I'm not even close to being popular or anything, and everyone keeps staring at me like I'm some fungus that crawled out of a swamp."

A strange look crosses his face that I can't decipher. "You think they're staring at you because they think you're a fungus that crawled out of a swamp?"

"I don't know," I say, puzzled over the odd look he's giving me. "I mean, they probably don't literally think I'm fungus. They definitely stare at me like I am, though."

"That's not why they're staring at you. I promise."

"Well, I wish they'd stop. It makes me feel self-conscious, and I've had way too much of that in my life. That's what I loved about being overseas. No one knew me, so I never had to worry about people making fun of me."

"No one's making fun of you," he says earnestly. "I'll see what I can do with the staring."

"What, are you going to ask the entire school to stop looking at me?" I ask jokingly, expecting him to laugh.

"I could do that. I think I'll try something else first," he says with a devious smile as he wiggles his brows at me.

"Don't do anything that'll make it worse," I beg, clasping my hands together. "Please, promise me you won't, Kai."

"Cross my heart and hope to die. Stick a needle in

Hannah's eye," he says then kisses the tip of my ear before letting me go.

I jolt from the weird kiss move, which only makes him laugh.

"Well, at least you think you're funny," I tease him.

"I *know* you think I'm funny, too." He picks up his half-eaten apple then flashes me his pearly whites. "It's why you're always laughing when you're around me."

I open my mouth to tease him, to tell him he's never funny, that I never, ever laugh at him, and that he should stop telling jokes all the time; but Kyler walks into the kitchen, wearing loose fitting basketball shorts and a tank top. And his hair is damp, like he just got out of the shower.

The only time I've seen him since I got back was when he was arguing with Hannah in the driveway, so being this close to him puts my love/lust meter into confusion mode.

I spent three months irritated with him, thinking he was dating Hannah. I thought I'd gotten over my crush on him. Then, I found out he was never really dating her, and now it's left me feeling more confused than ever.

Do I like him still?

Kinda, sorta, yeah.

"Hey, have you seen my gym bag?" Kyler asks Kai as he heads for the fridge. When he catches sight of me, he freezes, his brows pulling together. "Hey ..."

"Hey." I wince at the breathiness of my voice.

Get your shit together. Don't be nervous. You're not like that anymore. You kissed Nyle on the London Eye, for Christ's sake. And you're not even sure how you feel about him anymore.

Kyler seems to find my spasticness more amusing than repulsive and smiles at me.

I'm convinced he doesn't recognize me. He's never smiled at me like that before, not even when he gave me the rose or hung out with me while we played basketball.

The rose. The pity gift.

I frown, remembering what Hannah told me. Was there any truth to her words?

"Isa, why do you look like you just ate something sour?" Kai asks, yanking me back to reality.

"Because I did eat something sour," I lie.

Kai rolls his eyes. "Whatever."

"You look different, Isa," Kyler says, studying me from head to toe.

Well, at least he seems to know who I am.

"Um, thanks," I reply, unsure if different is a compliment or not.

"I don't mean that in a bad way," Kyler quickly explains. "I just mean that you look different. Good different, I promise." He smiles a smile that reaches his eyes.

I can't help smiling back and probably look as goofy as Goofy himself.

"Thanks," I tell him with more confidence.

His lips part, but Kai cuts him off.

"Your gym bag's in the car," he says coldly. "You left it there after practice, and Mom blamed it on me. I have no fucking clue why it's my responsibility to take care of your shit."

"She probably thought it was your bag," Kyler tells him, ripping his attention off me. "You always leave yours in there, and it stinks up the car."

"I haven't had a gym bag in almost a year." Kai reclines against the counter with his arms folded.

"I thought you were going to try to get back on the team this year?" Kyler asks, using his lean arms to reach up and open one of the top cupboards.

Kai shakes his head, annoyance flaring in his eyes. "That's Mom's wishful thinking. I'm not going to try out for the team. I have better things to do with my time."

"Like what?" Kyler grabs a box of protein bars before shutting the cupboard. "Get high and watch television?"

Okay, things are really starting to get awkward and uncomfortable. I'm deciding whether I should back out of the room and bail when Kyler turns to me.

"Sorry about that," he says. "We shouldn't be arguing like this in front of you."

Kai scowls at Kyler. "Why? She hears us all the time when she's out on her balcony listening to us."

"Hey." I shoot Kai a dirty look. "Way to throw me under the bus."

Kai looks a tab bit remorseful. "Sorry. He already knows you do it."

"It's okay," Kyler says to me, tucking the box under his arm. "I always thought it was kind of cute the way you watched us."

He may be trying to make me feel better, but I feel like a class-A freak right now.

"I have to get to practice." Kyler grabs a bottle of water out of the fridge then backs toward the washroom. "Isa?"

I gradually turn around to look at him. "Yeah?"

"You should come watch one of my games sometime." He flashes me a dimpled grin. "You could come cheer me on and bring me good luck. Like you did with my free throws."

I internally gag. Football. So gross and soooo boring. Seriously, I've been in the room while my dad's watched games and it's a yawn fest. I'd way rather spend my time reading, drawing, going to Comic-Con, getting my favorite books signed, or blogging. Hell, I'd take running to the paint store in my underwear over watching a bunch of dudes throw a ball around and tackle each other.

I'm not about to tell Kyler any of that. Not when he just invited me to go see him play. In public, and not just when we're at one of our houses where no one can see us.

I plaster on the fakest smile. "Sounds like super fun!" Okay, I might have gone a little overboard with the *super*.

Kyler grins, seeming oblivious to the fact I'm faking

my enthusiasm. "Awesome. There's one next Friday. Let me know if you need a ride." He winks at me like Kai does all the time.

I keep on smiling until he leaves the house then my head slumps forward, and my mouth falls open. "Holy shit."

Kai snorts a laugh. "Watching you try to sound happy about watching him play was seriously the most entertaining thing I've ever seen."

I sweep loose strands of my rain-kissed hair out of my face then turn to face him. "I hate football, okay? Honestly, I'm not a fan of watching any sport, period."

"But you play them." He opens the fridge and takes out two cans of Coke. "I remember you winning some sort of free throw contest or something."

"Playing sports and watching them are two totally different things." I catch a can of Coke as he tosses one to me. "I have a short attention span unless it involves books, writing, or drawing."

"I know you do," he says simply, popping the tab of the can open.

"How can you possibly know that about me?" I ask, opening my soda. "No one, except maybe my grandma, knows that about me."

He thrums his finger against his bottom lip. "Hmmm … Let me think. How on earth did I find out all that stuff about you …?" An impish grin plays at his lips. "There has to be some sort of online place where I read all about your interests. Oh, yeah, I remember now. There was this page that had all these thoughts of yours on it. There were also some pretty cool pictures of your trip that I didn't see on your phone."

I feel like I've entered *The Twilight Zone.*

"You were on my *blog!*" Shit. Did he read my last entry? If so, then he knows about my mom.

He shrugs like it's no biggie. "It's kind of interesting, and you're kind of funny."

"Gee, thanks," I say sarcastically. "And you're *kind of* nice."

"Why, thank you," he replies with over-exaggerated happiness.

I resist an eye roll then try to get a vibe from him; see if maybe he knows about my mom. Is there pity in his eyes? No, not really. If anything, he appears amused.

"When's the last time you were on it?" I ask. "My blog, I mean."

"I don't know, like, four or five days ago."

I exhale in relief. I made the post yesterday.

He winds around the kitchen island and heads for the doorway that leads to the living room. "Come on. I need to grab some stuff before I go to the party."

"I never said I was going."

It's not like I don't want to go to a party. I just worry that people from my school will be there, which means I'll end up spending the entire night avoiding their stares, probably hiding out in the bathroom.

He spins around, grinning. "Oh, come on. You know you want to go." His grin expands. "It'll be *super* fun!"

I flip him the middle finger, and he laughs.

"Besides, if you go, I can introduce you to some people from our school. Getting to know people is the first step to friendship." He grins.

"You would really do that for me?" I'm oddly touched.

He waves me off like it's no big deal. "I have excellent people skills. Stick with me and you will, too." Then he grabs my arm and pulls me with him, leaving me no choice but to go.

CHAPTER TWO

"I HAVE TO CHANGE BEFORE WE LEAVE," I ANNOUNCE TO Kai after he walks out of his bedroom, wearing different clothes.

He's now sporting a long-sleeved grey Henley, black jeans, and boots. He also has on a grey knit cap and a collection of leather bands on his wrist, including the one I gave him. I won't ever admit it to him aloud, but he looks dangerously sexy.

He evaluates me from head to toe while shoving up the sleeves of his shirt. "Why? You look fine." He tugs on the bottom of my still-damp tank top. "And I think a lot of people will probably appreciate the wet T-shirt look."

I fold my arms over my chest, mentally cursing myself when my cheeks go all melted chocolate warm.

Please don't notice I'm blushing. Please don't notice I'm blushing.

His lips spread into a grin. "The blush would be an added bonus, too. Between the T-shirt and that, you might be able to get free drinks all night."

I square my shoulders, scrounging up the little dignity I have left. "Bradon charges people for drinks at his parties? *Really?*"

"Not all the time, just sometimes." Kai nonchalantly shrugs. "He's an entrepreneur."

I run my hands over the front of my shirt. "As much as I'd love free drinks for the night, I think I'd rather wear some clean, more weather-appropriate clothes, and just pay if I drink."

"*If* you drink?" Kai questions with amusement. "You're a virgin drinker, aren't you?"

"Oh, please. You think I spent three months overseas and didn't touch a drink?" I scoff with a roll of my eyes. "I've drank a ton."

His lips twitch as he wrestles back a laugh. "Okay, I believe you. Just a warning, I'd stay away from any baked goods if I were you."

"Warning noted."

I can't believe I'm doing this—going to a party where I might run into people I know and that Kai is going to introduce me to. This will be so much different, and I'll be way more out of my element than when I was dancing in clubs and kissing guys I barely knew.

Before Kai and I leave, I go over to my house to change my clothes.

"You can just wait on the sofa, if you want," I tell him when Kai tags along with me as I head upstairs to my room.

"Nah, I'll just wait outside your bedroom door for you."

"You're such a weirdo."

"That's why we get along so well," he replies, grinning.

Smiling, I dash up the stairs and to my room. After I get the door shut, I head for the closet to pick out an outfit. As I pass by my bed, though, something catches my attention and makes me grind to a halt.

A piece of paper.

I pick it up off my bed, and my heart slams against my chest.

"Holy shit! Holy shit! *Holy shit!*"

Kai bursts in, wide-eyed and panicked. "What happened?"

"I don't ..." My hands and legs are shaking about as badly as my voice. I sink to the mattress, struggling to catch my breath. "It's nothing. I just found my birth certificate; that's all." When a pucker forms at his brow, I add, "I've been trying to find it for a week or so."

"Okay. I get where all the crazy was coming from now." A beat or two goes by as he glances from me to the paper in my hand then shifts his weight and cracks his knuckles.

"You read my post, didn't you?" I can read the truth all over his face, and by how twitchy he's acting. "Why didn't you say anything when we were in your kitchen?" I ask, pushing to my feet. "You said you hadn't read it in, like, four or five days."

"That was a guesstimate." He looks guilty. "And I was just saying what I felt like you wanted me to say. It didn't seem like you wanted me to know."

"I didn't. Not yet, anyway." Looking down at my birth certificate, my excitement bubble pops.

Where the mother's name is supposed to be is blank. But my father's is there in dark ink, a reminder that, yes, he may hate me, but I am his flesh and blood.

"So, does it say it?" Kai asks tentatively, leaning over to get a closer look at the certificate.

I lift my gaze to him. "Say what?"

"Who your mother is. That's why you were so excited to find it, right? Because you want to know who she is."

I really, really wish I would've gone with my gut instinct and deleted that post.

"Kai, you can't tell anyone about this, okay? My dad, he doesn't know I'm looking for her, and he got really upset when my grandma asked him about my mom."

"Does Lynn or Hannah know you're looking for her?" His voice conveys worry.

"I don't know." I glance down at the certificate again, and my good mood deflates even more as another thought occurs to me. This was the piece of paper in the photo the unknown caller sent to me. "Someone has to know, though." I bite on my lip as I mull it over. "The only person home right now is Hannah. I'm pretty sure she's the one who did it."

"You think Hannah put this on your bed?" Kai looks unconvinced. "I hate to say this, because I know it might hurt you, but why would Hannah try to help you?"

"Nothing you can say about Hannah will hurt me. I've pretty much developed an immunity to her bitchiness."

Kai presses his lips together as he stares at me with insinuation in his eyes.

"Why are you looking at me like that?" I ask. "I'm being serious. Hannah doesn't bother me anymore."

"Okay … It's just that I've been wondering if maybe your new hot girl look thingy has something to do with what I said to you before you left." He stuffs his hands in his pockets, tense as a tightly wound rope. "That this was your way of trying to get her to stop being mean to you all the time."

"That's not what that was about." My tone comes out more clipped than I want it to. I clear my throat. "My change was about me. I don't—didn't—even know who I was. And I wanted to figure that out."

"You're still kind of confused, it seems like," he accuses, carrying my gaze.

"Maybe a little." *Maybe a lot.*

With each passing day, I feel more lost as the possibility of finding my mom grows dimmer.

What if this is it for me? This lonely room with bare

walls and a family who loathes me. The idea is so depressing, so dream squashing. *No, I won't go there.*

"You know it's okay, right?" Kai says, scuffing the tip of his boot against the carpet as he stares down at the floor. "To be confused over who you are."

"Are you confused about who you are?" I don't really expect an answer, since he usually changes the subject whenever someone mentions his bad-boy makeover.

His gaze elevates to mine, and that let-me-hypnotize-you-with-my-eyes look is smoldering fiercely. "I was. It's actually getting clearer now, though," he says then immediately changes the subject. "Quick question. Why would Hannah put your certificate on your bed? Isn't that kind of, in a way, helping you find your mom? Because that doesn't seem like something Hannah would do."

"It's not really helping me since it doesn't have my mom's name listed. I mean, I already know her first name is Bella because my dad let it slip out to my grandma. And he was really mad when he did that." I blow out a stressed breath. "So either this is Hannah's way of rubbing in my face that I'm motherless, or maybe she thinks if she helps me find my mom, it'll get rid of me."

"Now *that* sounds like Hannah."

I chew on my bottom lip, debating if I should tell him about the text messages, too.

"I've been getting some weird texts … ever since I found out about my mom. They're from an unknown caller, but I'm pretty sure it's Hannah." I take out my phone and open up a message. "I got this message earlier today." I show Kai the photo the unknown caller sent me and the message. "I don't think anyone else besides Hannah could've gotten into the house, found my birth certificate, and put it on my bed."

With his brows dipped, Kai asks, "What about Lynn?"

"She's gone on a vacation with my dad."

He considers something with a torn look on his face.

"What's wrong?" I ask, putting my phone away.

"It's nothing … I'm just trying to figure out what the hell Hannah is up to."

"She's probably just trying to hurt me. She's always doing stuff like this."

He doesn't disagree and looks sort of guilty about something.

"I'm sorry, Isa. I really am." He blows an exhale then his gaze falls to my hand. He takes the certificate from me. "Mind if I hang on to this for a couple of days? I may know a guy who can help you with your search. I'm not sure what kind of information he needs, but I can give it a try."

"You know, this is the third time you've said something very mafia-ish to me," I point out. "You want to tell me something about you and these new friends of yours?"

"No way. That would take away all of my mystery." His lips quirk as he looks at me, and I can't help smiling despite all the crazy stuff going on in my life right now. "Then I'd just be boring Kai again."

"I kind of liked boring Kai." I playfully nudge his foot with mine. "Well, sometimes, anyway."

"You never really knew him, Isa. No one really did."

"I did a little, though."

"Maybe a little," he agrees, tucking the certificate into the back pocket of his jeans.

Well, I guess that's that.

It makes me nervous to think about what he's going to do with that piece of paper. Who's this guy he's going to talk to? And how can he find my mom without knowing more than her first name?

"Hurry and get changed. Let's hit up this party so we can relax." He backs toward the door, fishing his phone from his pocket. "And while you're doing that, I'm going to go have a little chat with Hannah and see if I can get to the bottom of this."

Confusion clouds my mind. "You'd do that for me?"

He shrugs. "Yeah, why not?" A smile touches his lips. "I'm always up for pissing Hannah off."

CHAPTER THREE

Kai's talk with Hannah doesn't go down the way he hoped. Apparently, all she wanted to do was flirt with him and talk about how hot she looked.

"God, she's so annoying," he gripes as we get into his car.

I giggle. "You just figured that out?"

He shakes his head. "No. I was just painfully reminded of it." He backs down the driveway toward the road. "Sorry, I couldn't get her to talk."

"That's okay." It's the truth, too. While I'd love for Hannah to confess she did it, I still ended up with my birth certificate.

"I did go through her phone to see if maybe she's just blocked her number and that's why it's coming up as unknown," Kai adds. "But either she's deleted all the texts and photos or she's sending them from another phone."

I give him a suspicious look. "How'd you get on her phone? She has a password."

He shrugs. "I have my ways." When I continue to stare at him, he sighs. "I'm kind of good at cracking people's passwords."

I wait for him to embellish. Instead, he turns up the radio and focuses on driving, leaving me to come up with my own assumptions.

THE HOUSE WHERE THE PARTY IS AT IS WAY THE HELL OUT near the foothills, about a thirty-minute or so drive from the suburbs where Kai and I live.

For the first half of the drive, Kai and I argue about what song we should listen to. He wants to turn on his party song, which is pretty much just bass and dirty lyrics. When he turns the song on, my ears groan in protest, and I reach forward and snatch up his iPod.

"Hey." Kai blasts me with a zombie rage, I'm-going-to-eat-your-brains-out look. "I know you're new to riding with me, so I'm going to tell you the rules as nicely as I can." He extends his hand over the console to steal the iPod away from me, but misses. "No one, under any circumstances, ever gets to touch my stereo."

Smirking, I line my back against the door so I'm out of his reach, quickly scrolling through his songs.

"Isa," he warns, his gaze dancing back and forth

between the road and me as he drives down the busy street. "I'm being serious. I have issues with music."

"Clearly." I snicker as I note some of the songs he has on the device. "Dude, your music taste sucks. What happened to that obsession with 80s punk music? There aren't any songs that are even close to punk."

"I go through music phases." His fingers tighten around the steering wheel as his expression darkens. "And I'm super touchy about people insulting my current music tastes." He suddenly relaxes, shaking and rolling out his shoulders. "You know what? I'm going to let that one slide just as long as you put the iPod down."

I quickly tap the folder labeled "For Your Eyes Only," click the first song, and set the iPod down. A song by Violent Soho flows through the speakers, and I smile.

"Okay, this one's not too bad."

"Whoa. Whoa. Whoa. You turned on one of my private songs," he says then grins and turns up the volume, singing along.

Private songs? God, I don't even want to know what he does when he listens to those.

I laugh at my own thoughts and end up doing an awesome snort.

"What's so funny?" Kai asks, giving me a curious, side-long glance.

I swiftly shake my head. "It's nothing."

A grin creeps up his face. "You were thinking something dirty, weren't you?"

"No, I was just thinking about … something."

"About something dirty with my private playlist."

I stick out my tongue at him, and he just laughs. Then I relax back in my seat and cross my legs, moving carefully since I'm wearing a skirt and don't want to flash him.

I matched the skirt with a long-sleeved black shirt, clunky black boots, and a studded leather jacket I bought in one of the shops on Oxford Street in London. I hope I look good enough for a party, but since I've never been to one, I'm unsure.

I run my fingers through my wavy hair, trying to add volume, being careful not to snag any of the braids.

"You look fine," Kai says, misreading my primping.

My hands fall to my lap. "I was just trying to make my hair bounce more."

He taps on the brakes to slow for a stoplight then twists in the seat, looking at me with his brow cocked. "Bounce? I didn't know hair bounced."

"Tell that to my cousin Indigo. She seems to think hair needs to bounce all the time."

"I'll never understand girls."

"And I'll never understand guys. It's like, one minute, you're sweet, and then the next, you're all like"—I drop my voice to a low baritone—" 'Whatever, I don't care about anything anymore.' "

"I always care about stuff," he says, driving forward as the light turns green. "Sometimes, I just can't show it."

"That's really silly."

"About as silly as pretending we were wizards."

"Hey, I was a witch." I smile as I remember how, during our walks home, we'd sometimes stop at the park and pretend we were awesome enough to possess the power of magic. "Not a wizard."

"Whatever. It was still silly. I mean, we were almost thirteen years old, for God's sake. We were too old to be playing make-believe." Though his eyes are glued to the road, I can sense the tension flowing off him.

"Well, I didn't. And I still don't think it's silly." I focus on the shops, the local bank, and the small grocery store lining the street, trying to ignore the pain over how he thinks our time together was silly—that I'm silly.

"You're still the same," he remarks. I can feel his eyes on me.

"I'm a little different," I reply without looking at him. "But yeah, I'm kind of the same, too."

"That's not a bad thing, Isa." He brushes his fingers right above my injured knee.

I jolt in the seat as his touch ripples across my body and zaps my heart like a defibrillator. *What in the wild, wild crazy land was that?*

"I know it's not a bad thing. I know I'm weird, and I've always been pretty okay with that. I just wish I knew why." An unsteady breath eases from my lips as I peek down at Kai's hand on my leg then over at him.

He quickly withdraws his hand and places it on the steering wheel. "Why what?"

"Why I am the way that I am. I've never fit in with anyone, especially my family. And then I found out that Lynn isn't my mom, and I kind of … I don't know … felt relieved, which probably makes me a bad person, but that's how I feel."

"That doesn't make you a bad person at all. I've heard some of Hannah's stories about the stuff they've done to you. You should hate her."

"She's told people about the things she's done to me?"

Nausea sets in as I think about all the incriminating pictures she snapped of me doing embarrassing, dorky things.

He offers me a look of empathy. "I'm sorry. I shouldn't have brought that up."

"It's fine." I scrape at the black nail polish on my fingernails. "Sometimes, I wonder if Hannah's always known that we don't have the same mom, and that's why she's always treated me so bad."

"Hannah treats you bad because she's a spoiled princess." Kai downshifts the car. "She's basically gotten everything she's wanted since we were kids."

"I know … I don't get why people even like her."

"Because they're afraid of her. They'd rather be her friend than her enemy."

"So, you were afraid of her, then?" I ask. "Because you liked her once."

"I never *liked* her." He grinds his teeth. "I told you I just hit on her because I knew Kyler had a thing for her and it would piss him off. There was never anything more to it."

"If Kyler had a thing for her, then why isn't he dating her anymore?" I attempt not to sound bitter and fail epically.

"He liked her when he was younger, but he grew out of it," he explains, making a right down a side road that weaves between the rolling foothills. "It's probably the one smart thing he's ever done in his life. The whole dating thing at the beginning of the summer pretty much happened only because Hannah's pushy as fuck when she wants something."

"I completely agree." I restrain a smile, though it's difficult when I just found out Kyler never really wanted to go out with Hannah. He was probably being nice.

"So, you're still obsessed with him, huh?" Kai asks, jostling me of my Kyler lust trance.

"What? No! I'm not …" My cheeks erupt in flames. Fortunately, it's dark enough that there's no way Kai can see my mortification.

"Relax, Isa." He pats my uninjured knee, all buddy-buddy-like. "It's not really that big of a secret."

I frown. "It makes me sound pathetic—obsessing over some guy for years, who I have no chance in hell of ever going out with."

"Why don't you have a chance?" he asks, genuinely baffled.

"Um, because I'm me."

"Yeah, so? He asked you to his football game, didn't he?"

"I guess he did." I replay the two-second conversation I had with Kyler, trying to remember if, when he asked me, he was sending out date vibes. I don't know since I have zilch experience in the boyfriend department. "You think he was asking me out?"

"Probably." Irritation creeps into his tone. "He's shallow enough that he would."

"Why would him asking me out make him shallow?" I ask, offended.

"Because he doesn't know you, which means he was only asking you out based on the fact that he thinks you're hot now."

"That's kind of harsh. Maybe he knows me and likes me."

"How could he possibly know you?" Kai asks, flipping the blinker. "You two haven't ever talked."

"We hung out a couple of times when I taught him how to improve his free throws, and he used to stop Hannah from picking on me," I tell him. "There was this one time when he even stopped his own friends from picking on me. A couple of his football buddies had me cornered because Hannah basically had a choke collar on them. He came up and said something about them being late for practice so they'd have to leave."

"He should have called them out on what they were doing, not just fed them a lame-ass excuse to make them stop without making himself look bad." He makes another turn, this time down a street lined with single-story, seventies-style homes.

"You didn't do that for me, either." I clench my hands into fists as they begin to tremble.

I hate memory lane. Let's not go there ever again.

"Yeah, well, I was a fucking asshole back then. Still am most of the time. I don't want to be when I'm around you, though." He parks the car along the curb at the end of a very long line of vehicles. "My brother, on the other hand, walks around pretending he's all high and mighty, when really, he's a fucking arrogant prick who always puts himself first."

He slides the keys out of the ignition. "You may not want to believe this, but you're too sweet and smart for Kyler. It'll never work out." He shoves open the door to get out. "He'd be better off with your sister. The two of them are pretty much the same, except your sister doesn't give a shit that people think she's a douche."

With that, he climbs out of the car, leaving me to wonder if he's right. Could Kyler really be the asshole Kai seems to think he is?

CHAPTER FOUR

I'VE SEEN A TON OF MOVIES THAT FEATURED HIGH SCHOOL parties. I figured the rowdy, loud music and tons of people crammed into a house were Hollywood's played-up versions. When I catch sight of the single-story home the party is taking place at, though, I start to think the movies nailed it dead-on.

The small living room is jam-packed with sweaty, unruly, stupidly silly drunk people. Music is booming and vibrates the floors. The smell of sweat, beer, and cigarette smoke laces the air. And I'm pretty sure I just stepped in a puddle that I think might be urine.

"Ew!" I shiver as I stare down at the yellow puddle on the linoleum floor.

I'm distracted just long enough by the grossness that when I look up, I've lost Kai in the crowd. I stand on my tiptoes, panicking as my gaze surfs the crowd. There are just too many people to tell who's who.

"I'm never going to find him." Those old feelings of ridicule sneak up on me, and I hug my arms around myself, noting every glance in my direction.

They have to be staring at me. And you want to know why, Isabella? Because they know you don't belong here.

"Hey, I know you, right?" Bradon, Kai's friend and the guy throwing this shindig, stumbles through the crowd and stops in front of me. He has overly long hair, his eyes are red, and his clothes smell like smoke with a kick. "You're that chick from my school."

I want to point out there are a lot of chicks who go to our school here, but I'm guessing I'll probably just confuse him.

"Yeah, sure."

"You know Kai, right?" He wags a finger at me. "You're that girl who was by his locker."

Great. I went from being That Chick at School to being That Girl by Kai's Locker.

I stick out my hand to properly introduce myself so he'll stop giving me lame nicknames. "I'm Isa."

He eyeballs my hand, then wraps his fingers around mine, brings them to his lips, places a kiss on my skin, and then licks me like a dog.

I screech, loud enough to make a scene, and people glance our way. Apparently, drunk people have a short attention span, though, because five seconds later, they're all doing their own thing again.

"Sorry. I couldn't help it." He laughs at me as I wipe my hand on the side of my skirt. "I've never had a girl try to shake my hand before."

"If it happens again, you should probably just shake it back," I offer.

"Thanks. I'll keep that in mind." He noticeably checks me out before peering around the crowd. "So, did Kai come with you or what?"

I inch forward as a guy staggers past me and jabs his elbow into my back. "Yeah, he did. I don't know where he is, though. I lost him the second I walked in here."

"Yeah, that happens a lot." He looks back at me. "How about I help you find him?"

I nod, my anxiety going down a drop or two. "That sounds great. Thank you."

"No problem." He nods for me to follow him as he pushes his way through the crowd. "We can get you a brownie from the kitchen, too." He throws me a toothy smile from over his shoulder. "I make killer fudge brownies. They're actually pretty famous."

"I bet they are," I remark, remembering Kai's warning to stay away from the baked goods. "I actually don't like brownies that much." *Huh? Never thought that sentence would ever come out of my mouth.*

"That's because you haven't ever tasted mine." He raises his voice as an upbeat song blasts through the speakers, and everyone gets all riled up. "One bite will change your mind."

As I get jostled all over the place by the crowd, I thank the heavens that I'm wearing boots; otherwise, I'd be knocked flat on my ass by now. Heels were never my thing, something I learned every time I tried to wear them out to a club. I'd either trip, fall down completely, or my feet would end up hurting so badly that I'd have to sucker Indigo into swapping shoes. The only ones I can tolerate are platforms, but after wearing them to school last week, I've decided they might be as demonic as stilettos.

I struggle to maintain my balance, and Bradon snags my arm and tugs me out of the room, only letting me go when we make it safely into the kitchen. There are a few people hanging around a keg, but other than that, the room's pretty empty.

"Brownie time," Bradon announces as he lifts a paper towel off a plate.

Underneath it are the gooiest and most delicious looking brownies I've ever seen, and my mouth starts to salivate.

Bradon picks up the plate and moves it toward me. "Try one. I promise you won't regret it."

I literally have to stab my nails into my palms just to stop myself from snatching one and gobbling it up. "I can't."

"Why not?"

"Well, because … they have pot in them, right?"

He chuckles at me. "You're adorable. I can see why Kai likes you."

Before I can even wrap my head around what he said, an arm drops down on my shoulders.

"There you are," Kai says casually, though I can feel the tension in his arm. "I look away for, like, a second and you disappear on me. What happened?"

"I stepped in piss and got distracted," I explain, glancing down at my boot. "Or, at least I think it was piss."

Bradon puts a finger to his lip, seeming way too fixated on me. "Seriously adorable."

Kai gives me a questioning look. "How did you end up with Bradon?"

I lean in, keeping my voice low. "He found me in the crowd, licked my hand when I tried to introduce myself, then brought me in here, offered me a brownie, and called me adorable when I asked him if there was pot in it. I don't know why. I haven't done anything that could remotely constitute being called adorable."

Kai presses his lips together as he angles his head so he can look me in the eye. "You asked him if his brownies had pot in them?" he asks, struggling not to laugh.

"Why is that so amusing?" I feel like the butt of a joke I don't get. "You told me not to eat them because they have pot in them, right? I just wanted to make sure."

Kai glances at Bradon, who's still staring at me like I've sprouted a unicorn horn out of my forehead.

"Can I borrow her for the night?" Bradon asks Kai, his bloodshot eyes drinking in my every move.

"I'm not on loan," I quip then shrug. "Sorry."

Kai chokes on a laugh while Bradon blinks at me, confounded.

"Okay, how about we go get you something to drink?" Kai says to me, steering me across the kitchen and away from Bradon.

Once we reach the counter lined with all sorts of differently shaped alcohol bottles, he lifts his arm from my shoulders.

"So, what's your drink?" He holds up his hands. "No, wait a minute; let me guess. A wine cooler."

"I've never had a wine cooler before," I admit.

"Then what did you drink when you were overseas?" He reaches for a bottle filled with red liquid that has tiny little flakes at the bottom, picks it up, pulls a face, and then sets it down.

"Lots of stuff. Whenever we'd do shots, though, Indigo would always make us do vodka." I shudder, remembering the scorching burn.

Kai muses over something then moves for the fridge. When he returns, he has a beer in his hand. "How about a beer? I don't think it'll make you pull that face you just made when you mentioned vodka."

I gratefully take the beer and twist the cap off while

Kai grabs a plastic cup and fixes himself a drink using soda and whiskey.

"Now what do we do?" I ask as he screws the cap back on the whiskey.

"Whatever you want." He downs a large swallow from his cup.

I smile artfully at him. "Okay, well, if that's the case, then I want to chase a unicorn, run on a rainbow, and swim in a lake made of gold."

He rolls his eyes at me, a smile playing at the corners of his lips. "We can do whatever you want within the realm of reality."

"Reality's no fun." I pout.

"That's not true," he says, his gaze drifting across the room. "I bet you've had fun in reality before."

"Yeah, I guess." I sip my beer, remembering the time I probably had the most fun. "I did have a lot of fun on my trip."

"Okay, that's a starting point." He swishes around his cup. "What did you do on the trip that was so fun?"

I shrug. "I don't know. I saw a ton of cool stuff and did a crap load of crazy things. You saw the pics on my blog, right?"

"I saw the pics," he says. "But I want to know about these so-called crazy things you did. Because a lot of those photos were of places, not you."

"We did a lot of stuff. I guess one of my favorite things was when we went clubbing."

His brows shoot up. "You went clubbing?"

"You don't have to sound so shocked about it." I chug down half my beer as my social anxiety jumps onstage and takes over like a puppet. I know it's insane, but it feels like his surprise screams, *"You don't belong here!"*

"I'm sorry," he tells me sincerely. "You just threw me off. I mean, the Isa I knew didn't dance."

"Well, she can dance now." I straighten my shoulders as the beer swims through my veins. "And let me tell you, she's *awesome.*"

"Is that so?" he remarks, rubbing his jaw.

I cringe, seeing where he's heading with this. "Yeah, but only when I'm in clubs."

He nods toward the living room where people are packed together like sardines, grinding together like they've been drinking liquid hormones. "This place is kind of club-ish."

"Not really." I fight back the panic strangling my throat. "Kai, please don't make me dance in front of all these people. I know some of them."

"It'll be fine. I'll even dance with you." He guzzles down a huge mouthful of his drink, tosses the cup into the garbage, threads his fingers through mine, and then hauls me toward the living room.

Before we dive head-on into the dancing orgy, Kai lets go of me and walks over to the stereo system in the corner of the room. Bradon is sitting near it, sipping on a drink. When Kai approaches him and says something, Bradon makes a face and promptly shakes his head.

"No way!" Bradon shouts, standing to his feet and placing himself in front of the stereo. "That'll never happen, dude."

"Oh, come on!" Kai begs, reaching for the stereo. "Just let me do it."

Bradon swats his hand away. "You know I don't take requests like that unless it's from a hot chick."

Kai throws a quick glance at me then leans in and says something to Bradon. I don't know what he's saying, but I have a feeling he might be using me to get his song request past Bradon.

Bradon frowns then reclines back over the table and presses a few buttons before he sits up. The room grows quiet, and people immediately start complaining.

"Turn the fucking music on!" a lanky guy not too far away from me hollers.

"Bradon, quit being a dick!" a girl wearing a flowing floral dress shouts, red-faced and pissed as hell.

"You owe me, dude," Bradon grumbles as Kai struts back toward me.

He gives him a thumbs up without turning around, walking right for me.

"All right, it's dancing time," he says, rubbing his hands together.

"What'd you get him to turn on?" I ask before the song

clicks on, and I have my answer. I giggle. "You picked a Katy Perry song?"

"What? She rocks!" he replies, owning his song choice. He snatches hold of my hand and drags me through the people who've started dancing again. "Now, come on; you owe me a dance."

"How do you figure that?" I stumble after him as he shoves his way to the center of the room.

He elbows people out of the way to clear some space then his fingertips press down on my wrist before he spins me around so my back is aligned with his chest. "Because you never gave me the wand you promised me."

I start to laugh then stop myself. "You never gave me a chance to give you the wand. Three days after I promised you I'd make you one, you decided you were too cool to walk home with me anymore."

"I came to your house after that happened," he says. "You could've given it to me then."

I tip my chin up to look at him. "When did you come to my house?"

"After I told my friend you were stalking me." Remorse fills his eyes. "I wanted to say sorry. I know it wouldn't have meant much since I wasn't planning on telling people the truth, but I felt bad."

"Why didn't I know you stopped by?"

"Probably because Hannah answered the door and I chickened out."

The mention of Hannah painfully reminds me of the

birth certificate and how she probably put it on my bed for me to find. If she's trying to get rid of me, then that's probably the tip of the iceberg. Who knows what other kinds of mean games are waiting for me at home?

"Stop overthinking and dance." He grinds his hips against my backside, and I laugh, finding it funnier than I probably should.

But this is Kai, not some random stranger at a club who Indigo roped into dancing with me. Kai, who used to walk home with me, who secretly shared my love for magic, superheroes, and zombies. Who teases me constantly and pisses me off sometimes.

He seems pretty adamant about dancing with me, though, upping his moves as he grips my hips and pulls me closer.

"Okay, I guess we're doing this, then." I down the rest of my beer, knowing I'm going to need it, then set the empty bottle down on the floor.

Giving one final panicked glance at the people around me, I sway my hips and rock to the beat. I don't move slowly, either. That's not my style. I may have social anxiety, but give me a drink and some loud music, and I'll go wild. I'm talking freak out, lose your mind, whip it, shake your groove thang kind of dancing. I blame it on Indigo and the first time we went out clubbing.

Kai slides his hand around to my waist, his fingers dipping under the hem of my shirt. When his knuckles graze my bare skin right above my hipbone, I have a hard time focusing. And breathing. Suddenly, I no longer think dancing with him is that funny. I find it ... well, sexy.

He traces circles on my skin as he grinds his hips against me, and I fight to keep moving the way I was before all the touching started. I keep spacing out and forgetting how to function.

His breath caresses my ear as he chuckles. "You seem tense. I thought you said you could dance."

He's so doing this on purpose to distract me.

"Yep, I sure can," I say, and then really start dancing, ignoring everything around me like I did when I was overseas.

I lift my arms, sway my hips, and rock out, matching the beat of the song. Kai lines his body up with mine, and we move together perfectly. Song after song, we keep going, practically having sex with our clothes on. I'd be embarrassed—and maybe I will be come morning. As of right now, I'm having fun.

I'm not sure how long we dance or how long it would've gone on, but Kai ruins the moment by licking the side of my neck.

I squeal, whirling toward him while I wipe his slobber off my neck.

He gives me an innocent look. "What? That's how I thought all the cool kids were greeting each other tonight."

I keep my hand cupped over the side of my neck for

protection. "First of all, you weren't trying to greet me. And second of all, it creeped the hell out of me when Bradon did it."

His chest shakes as he fights not to laugh at me. "I don't think I'm as creepy as Bradon."

"You know what? You're right." Which means I can pay him back.

I let my arm fall to the side, lean forward, and lick his neck like a dog.

He jumps back, startled, and then busts up laughing, hunching over as he grasps his side. Unable to help myself, I join in with him.

After the laughter dies down, we mutually agree not to lick each other anymore and start dancing and drinking again. By the time we stop to get some water, we're sweaty, hot, and out of breath.

We wander back into the kitchen where Kai gets a bottle of water from the fridge, taking a sip before handing it to me. I down most of it in just a few gulps then hand the bottle back to him.

"Now you've got me curious," Kai says after he finishes the rest of the water.

"Over what?" I ask, wiping my damp forehead with my hand.

"Who taught you how to dance like that?"

"That awesomeness can't be taught. It's just pure talent."

Chuckling, he fixes himself another drink, this time

mostly whiskey and a splash of soda. "All right, you own your awesomeness."

I smile as he hands me a beer. I open the bottle then trail after him as he glides the sliding glass door open and ducks outside onto the back patio.

The crisp night air feels great on my sweaty skin as I step outside. I figure the reason Kai came out here was to get some fresh air, but he continues down the steps and heads toward a pool house in the far back corner of the yard.

Unsure if he wants me to follow him, I lollygag on the patio, keeping my distance from a couple of guys lounging in the lawn chairs, smoking and laughing about something.

"You coming? Or are you just going to stand there?" Kai hollers when he stops in front of the pool house door, the porch light hitting his face.

Relieved he isn't making me stand there by myself, I hurry down the stairs and across the grass to him, gulping down my beer.

"I wasn't sure if you wanted me to follow you or not," I say, picking at the label on the beer bottle.

"Silly girl, of course I wanted you to follow me," he replies, his speech starting to slur.

I laugh at him. "You're so drunk."

"No way," he insists, stumbling and bumping his elbow on the door. He blinks as he looks inside his cup. "Okay, maybe just a little."

He sets his cup down on a rusty patio table, raises his hand, and taps his knuckles against the door.

"What are we doing out here?" I put the mouth of the bottle to my lips and take another drink.

A drunkenly droopy grin spreads across his face that makes him so adorably cute it's ridiculous. "This is my connection." He pats the door like it's his best friend.

I lower the bottle from my mouth. "Connection?"

He pats the back pocket of his jeans where my birth certificate is tucked away. "This is where my guy is."

I stare at the rotting wooden door. "Your guy lives in Bradon's pool house?"

"No, he just chills here a lot."

"Um, okay."

"It's not as sketchy as it sounds."

"Good. Because it sounds pretty damn sketchy."

"I would never let anything happen to you." He drapes his arm around my shoulders, and I get a whiff of his whiskey breath. "Remember the cave?"

It takes me a moment or two to sort through my beer-laced thoughts and figure out what he's talking about. Back when we hung out, we found this hollowed out tree we nicknamed "the cave," where nothing bad could ever happen to us.

"When I'm in the cave, my sister Hannah and my mom can't see me," I said as I slid inside the hollow trunk. "And maybe my dad can."

"When I'm in the cave, I get to be me," Kai said as he

ducked in behind me. "No one else, including my mom or dad, can try to make me be anyone else."

"And we have to promise never to tell anyone about this place." I hugged my knees to my chest to make room for his gangly legs.

He bent awkwardly until he fit inside. "It's a deal."

"Cross your heart." I traced an X across my heart. "Hope to die. Stick a needle in Hannah's eye."

He laughed at me and sketched an X across his chest. "I promise."

"I wonder if the tree's still there," I say with a trace of a smile.

"It is," Kai assures me, averting his gaze from mine.

"How do you know?"

"Because I sometimes go there to think."

"Really? That's … kind of nice, I guess."

He shrugs, staring at the ground. "You should also know that I sometimes get high there, too."

I crinkle my nose. "So, you do get high?"

"Not for a while, but yeah, if we're totally being honest, I did it a handful of times over the summer."

"But you seemed so irritated over people accusing you of doing drugs."

"I was irritated." His jaw clenches. "I know it's not an excuse, but I was going through some shit, and it was the only way to clear my head."

"Are you still going through some shit?" I blame the beer for asking the question.

He parts his lips to answer when then the door swings open, and relief washes over his face as he turns away from me.

"Kai, what's up, man?" A large guy wearing a backward baseball cap, netted shorts, and a stained white shirt stands in the doorway with his fist extended toward Kai.

Kai bumps knuckles with him.

"Not much. Just came to see what's been going on."

"Not a whole fucking lot," the guy replies, leaning against the doorjamb. "Business has been super fucking slow."

"That sucks, man," Kai says. "I might have a little business for you."

"Really?" The guy rubs his goatee. "What kind of business are we talking about?"

Kai glances at me from the corner of his eye, and the guy tracks his gaze. Even with the beer in my system, I still squirm as he scrutinizes me.

"Who's your friend?" he asks Kai, giving a chin nod in my direction.

I shyly wave back.

"This is Isa." Kai drags his hand over his head, tugging off his knitted cap. He ruffles his fingers through his hair, causing the strands to go askew. "She's actually the one who's in need of your ever-so-awesome services."

"Is that so?" he asks thoughtfully.

I smile warily, unsure what to say. Kai hasn't even told me who this guy is or what his services are, and it feels like I have a bundle of crazed-out monkeys inside my tummy.

"She cool?" he asks Kai, straightening his stance.

"Yep. I'll even vouch for her," Kai says, crossing his arms.

Okay, I don't care what he says. Kai is *so* in the mafia.

The guy mulls it over a second or two then sticks out his hand toward me. "Isa, I'm Big Doug."

"It's nice to meet you, Big Doug." I take his hand and shake it, hoping he doesn't lick me like Bradon did.

"My pleasure. My pleasure." His hand dwarfs mine as he gives it a soft squeeze. Then he pulls away, moves back, and motions for us to come inside. "Welcome to my paradise."

Big Doug's paradise consists of four brick walls, a floor cluttered with boxes, old candy wrappers, soda cans, and a table covered in computer screens, wires, modems, and all sorts of electronic stuff I know I've never seen before.

"Are you a hacker or something?" I don't mean to say it aloud. I slap my hand over my mouth, worried I've crossed a line.

Luckily, Big Doug seems fine with it.

"Hacking's just one of my talents." He waddles over to the table, kicking trash out of the way. Facing us, he sits down on the edge of the table. "But the question is … what talent do you want? Because I got a lot. All cost money, of course. I take cash or credit, depending on how well I know you."

Suddenly, the whole cracking into passcodes thing makes more sense.

My gaze slides to Kai and he shrugs, like *what?* I want to ask him so many questions, starting with how he knows a hacker. I'm not about to ask in front of Big Doug, though.

"Just put it on my tab." Kai places a hand on the small of my back, trying to reassure me. "You know I'm good for it."

Tab? Huh?

"Oh, okay. I didn't realize this was your thing." Big Doug stares at me just long enough to make me squirm. Then he fastens his attention on Kai. "So what's the job?"

Kai retrieves my birth certificate from his pocket and hands it over, giving Big Doug a quick explanation of what's going on.

"I was hoping you could take a look at the certificate and see if it's a fake or not," Kai says when he finishes explaining about my mom. "And if it is, I was hoping you'd have a couple of ideas on how to track her mom down."

Big Doug fiddles with the corner of the certificate. "All you know is that her name's Bella?" he asks, and Kai nods. "And your father's name is Henry Anders, right?" This time, he directs his question at me.

I nod, crossing my fingers he'll do this. This may be

illegal, but it still seems way less terrifying than asking my dad.

"I have one question before I agree to do this," Big Doug says to me. "Why not just ask your dad who she is?"

"Because he doesn't want me to know, for some reason," I explain. "I didn't even know about her up until a few months ago."

"Are you even sure she's alive?" he asks, setting the certificate down on the table beside one of the computers.

I shake my head, folding my arm around my waist as my gut twists into knots. "I don't know anything other than I lived with her for the first few years of my life before I went to live with my dad. And her name is Bella."

He bobs his head up and down. "Okay, give me a couple of weeks, and I'll see what I can come up with."

"Thanks, man," Kai says, sticking out his fist again.

The two of them bump knuckles again, and then Kai and I head out the door.

I don't say anything else until we reach the back patio. The guys who were there earlier have abandoned the lawn chairs, and the entire area is quiet.

"Okay, what the hell was that?" I spin around to face Kai, spreading my arms out to the side.

"What do you mean, *what the hell was that?*" Kai stares up at the stars. "That was me helping you out."

"That was some sketchy stuff. And how do you even know Big Doug?"

"I met him through Bradon. Did a little work for him a while back." He's still transfixed by the stars, so I pinch his arm to get him to look at me. "Ow." He chuckles, meeting my gaze as he laughs. "What was that for?"

"I just want to know that you're not going to get into trouble for that," I say, putting my hands on my hips.

"Why would I get in trouble? Big Doug's the one doing all the work." He reaches forward and slips his fingers through mine, moving my hand away from my hip. "Now, let's go inside and celebrate."

"Celebrate what?" I stare at our interlaced hands, confused over why he keeps touching me and why I feel comfortable with it.

"That in a week, you'll know who your mom is." He pulls me toward the door.

I let him steer me back inside, crossing my fingers that he's right and that Big Doug will be able to find my mom.

What I really hope is that she'll be alive when I do find her.

CHAPTER FIVE

TWO SHOTS AND A BEER LATER, I'M HEADING OUTSIDE TO wait for Indigo to come pick mine and Kai's sorry drunk asses up.

"You feeling better about going to school now?" Kai asks as we reach the curb. He spent the last three hours introducing me to everyone.

While I don't have anyone I'd call my best friend, I do feel better about going to school. And no one brought up the mental institution thing, so I'm guessing they all forgot about that rumor.

"Yeah. Thanks for introducing me to so many people," I say through a yawn.

"I feel bad I didn't do it sooner."

"I don't blame you. It's not like I'm the kind of person everyone wants to get to know. I'm too weird, and hardly anyone gets me."

"Isa, you're ridiculously freakin' awesome. Everyone who gets to know you is lucky."

"You're sweet when you're drunk," I tease with a nudge of my elbow.

"I'm always sweet when I'm around you, baby." He giggles.

I giggle, too. "You're a cheesy drunk." I yawn again, leaning against Kai, my eyelids feeling heavy. "I shouldn't have drunk so much."

"Just focus on that firefly over there." He points across the street at a glowing light. "It makes it easier to keep your eyes open."

I giggle again. "Kai, that's not a firefly. That's a porch light."

He leans all of his weight against me, nearly making me topple to the ground. "Hold me up, or I'm going to fall."

"You're a guy," I whine, digging my feet into the ground to support his weight. "You're supposed to hold me up."

"That's very sexist of you, Isa." He tsks, waving his finger at me. "I'm so disappointed."

I shake my head, a smile tickling at my lips. "Jesus, you're a handful."

"I know." He sighs tiredly. "If only I were like Kyler, then life would be so much easier for me and everyone around me."

My muscles ravel into knots as I stiffen, sensing a

drunken talk coming. You know the kind, when you yammer and pour your heart out with someone then, when you sober up, you have an oh-God-what-have-I-done moment.

"Kai, you're a good guy, no matter what you think."

"Yeah, tell that to my parents. Or my grandparents. Everyone in the entire Meyers family."

"Parents can suck, but that doesn't mean you have to believe everything they try to stick in your head. You're free to think whatever you want about yourself. Trust me."

"You wouldn't say that if you knew everything I did. I'm not a good person. I've done so much fucked up stuff."

"Everyone's done fucked up stuff," I say, shutting my eyes, wondering what he's done. Why he thinks he's so bad. "It doesn't make you a bad person. You just need to forgive yourself."

"Easier said than done." He yawns, sinking to the ground and clumsily pulling me with him.

I trip over his feet, and his fingers delve into my skin as he tries to stop me from falling. Still, we end up going down hard and landing in the grass in a tangle of legs and arms.

"Kai, you're the clumsiest drunk ever!" I laugh, trying to push him off me.

"Don't lie. I'm the funniest drunk ever." He laughs—

well, more like drunkenly giggles—as he rolls off me and onto his back. "And you're the cutest drunk ever."

"I so am not." I lie down with him so our heads, arms, and legs are touching. I look up at the stars twinkling in the sky, like handfuls of magic pixie dust. "And you wouldn't say that if you saw some of the stuff I did when I was in Scotland."

"Enlighten me, then." He tucks his arm under his head then looks at me.

"No way." I keep my eyes on the stars.

"Come on. Just one tiny thing, and then I'll let it go."

"Yeah, right. I'm learning you're the kind of person who doesn't just let things go."

"That does kind of sound like me," he agrees then reaches over and tickles my side.

"Kai!" I erupt in a fit of giggles. "Stop with the tickling!"

"No way." He travels downward to the bottom of my shirt and his sneaky little fingers dip under the fabric. He tickles me on my bare belly, which feels ten times worse, yet somehow ten times better. "It's too much fun watching you laugh."

"You're evil!"

"I know. You're the hero, and I'm the villain, right?"

"Yep! But you'll never win." I flip onto my stomach, ungracefully push to my feet, and skitter away from him.

He stands up, too, although it takes him a few attempts to get his feet under him. Then he moves toward me with his hands up but grinds to a halt as a group of older guys stroll across the grass toward us.

"Hey, Kai. How's it going, man?" one guy asks, and not in a friendly kind of way.

Kai tenses by my side. "T, what's up? I didn't know you were going to be here."

"Of course I'd be here. There's no way I was going to miss a chance to pay a visit to my friend." He says *friend* like it's a foul word.

I squint through the dark, trying to see what the guy looks like, but I've got my drunk beer goggles on.

"Who's this?" T asks Kai, smiling in my direction.

Kai grabs my arm and pulls me behind him. "What do you want?"

"I just wanted to pay you a visit," T says. "Make sure you haven't forgotten the deal."

"I haven't," Kai replies through gritted teeth.

Before anyone can say anything else, a car stops in the middle of the road and beeps the horn several times. I'm so relieved to see Indigo, and not just because I missed her. This T guy is giving me the heebie-jeebies.

"That's Indigo." I grab Kai's hand before I step off the curb, mostly because I'm worried he's going to fall.

"I'll be in touch," T calls out to Kai as I open the back door of the car.

"Who was that?" I ask as I help Kai get into the backseat.

"Just some dude who thinks he's the shit," he says tightly.

I know there's more to the story, but now's not the time to press him, especially with T still watching us.

I shut the door and slide into the passenger seat.

"Having fun?" Indigo asks with an insinuating smirk. She has on her pajamas, her hair is braided back, and she's wearing her square-framed reading glasses.

I buckle my seatbelt and tell Kai to put on his.

"It was just a party. No biggie."

"Sure it wasn't." Indigo shifts the car and drives forward, glancing in the rearview mirror at the backseat. "So you're Kai, huh?"

Kai, who seems to have gotten a second burst of energy, scoots forward in the seat and rests his arms on the console. "Yep, the one and only. The question is, how did you know that?" He eyes her over suspiciously.

"Isa told me about you," she says, pulling out onto the main road. "And I saw some of the texts you sent her while we were on our trip."

As his gaze glides to me, he props his elbow onto the console and rests his chin on his hand. "You've been telling people about me, huh?"

"Don't get too excited. I just told her about my annoying next-door neighbor; that's all."

I blast Indigo with a warning look, silently begging her to keep quiet.

"I'm not lying for you." She laughs as she reaches for the knob on the stereo. "So don't look at me like that."

A lazy grin expands across Kai's face. "What have you been saying about me? I want to know."

"I'm sure you do." I slip off my boots and prop my feet onto the dash, wiggling my toes.

He sticks out his bottom lip and flutters his eyelashes at me. "Pretty please?"

I shake my head. "No way."

"Oh, come on." He pouts. "Most girls fall for that look all the time."

"Ah-ha! I knew you did that on purpose to try to get your way." I point at him. "It's not going to work on me. I'm not like most girls."

"I know you're not." He turns dead serious. "And that's such a good thing. Seriously. We should hang out all the time. It's just too much fun with you."

"Isa, he's totally adorable." Indigo practically swoons in her seat.

"Hey, what a freakishly awesome coincidence," Kai says, sitting up straight. "My friend calls you adorable. Yours calls me adorable. We should be adorable together."

"Aw," Indigo says, pressing her hand to her heart.

"Don't *aw* anything he says," I tell her. "He doesn't even know what he's saying. He's too drunk."

"I am not," he says as his eyelids start to drift shut, validating my point.

"I don't care if he's drunk or not. He's a cutie, Isa." She

slows down for a stop sign and twists the stereo knob, surfing through the stations.

I peek back at Kai, who's already dozing off, his head tipped back. He's making this funny bubbling noise with his lips. He looks like a goof, but ...

"Okay, he's a little bit cute, but in a goofy way."

"So are you." She smiles at me. "But that's why I love you."

Kai suddenly wakes up, bounces forward, and slams his hand against the console. "Holy crap. Turn this shit up!"

Indigo leaves the radio on the station and cranks up the volume. A pop song I'm vaguely familiar with flows through the speakers and the bass booms.

Kai and Indigo start singing, bobbing their heads, and shimmying their shoulders.

"Well, at least you two share the same taste in bad music!" I laugh.

They look ridiculous, and I love them for it.

"Isa's kind of a music snob," Kai remarks between lyrics.

"Don't let her fool you," Indigo says then belts out more lyrics as she drives through the intersection. "She knows this song." She reaches over and pinches my side. "Come on, Isa, sing it." When I shake my head, she pinches me again. "Do it, do it ..."

Kai chants with her until finally I throw up my hands, surrendering.

"Fine! Only because I can't take the peer pressure."

The three of us sing and dance together, creating a sound that kind of resembles a herd of dying cats. By the time the song is finished, Kai is passed out in the backseat.

"I'm really glad you called me tonight," Indigo says as she steers the car through the sleepy town of Sunnyvale toward my subdivision.

"I promised you I'd never drink and drive or get into a car with someone who has been drinking," I tell her, resting my head back against the seat.

"That's not the only reason I'm glad." She flips the blinker on and changes lanes. "I tried to call you tonight after you sent me that text about getting another message from that unknown person. Are you okay?"

I nod then give her a quick recap of what happened today. By the time I'm finished, she looks fuming mad.

"I'm starting to wonder if maybe this isn't Hannah," she says. "I mean, the whole thing seems a little too smart for her.

"That thought's crossed my mind, too. If it's not her, though, then who could it be?"

Worry masks her expression. "Maybe Lynn ... or your dad."

Although the thought has briefly crossed my mind, I ask, "Why would my dad do this?"

She grows more concerned. "Maybe he thinks he's

scaring you enough that you'll stop looking for your mom."

"Then why would he leave my birth certificate on my bed?" I point out. "Besides, he's not even here. He's gone on a vacation with Lynn."

"Oh." She ponders something then shakes her head. "I have to tell you something else—or show you something, anyway. And I'm not sure how you're going to take it."

"Okay …?" Nervousness bubbles inside me.

"I found a box while I was going through some of Grandma Stephy's old stuff," she says as she pulls into my driveway. All the lights in the house are off, which hopefully means Hannah isn't home. "It has your dad's name on it, and I think I found something you might want." After she pushes the shifter into park, she opens the console, takes out a crinkled photo, and hands it to me.

The picture is of a woman holding a little girl, probably around two or three years old, and they're smiling at something in the distance. They have the same blue eyes and brown hair, looking similar enough that they could be mother and daughter.

"Who is this? Wait. You think …?" I blink at Indigo. "You think this is my mom and me?"

"I'm not sure, but I wonder if it might be. I don't even think your dad knows the photo was in the box. It was rolled up and stuck inside the bottom of a lamp. I actually thought it was a joint at first, but then I pulled it out and …" She trails off, staring at the closed garage door. "It was so weird how it was put in there, almost like someone hid it."

"Maybe my dad did it," I say quietly. "Maybe he wanted to keep something of my mother's and didn't want Lynn to know about it."

"Maybe. Or maybe your mom put it in there for you to find."

"That sounds like a huge stretch. How would my mom even get a lamp into a box of my dad's old stuff? It doesn't make any sense."

Her gaze glides to me. "I asked Grandma Stephy why the box was there, and she said your dad asked her to store it for her."

"Which means he probably put it there." I look down at the photo and swallow hard. We look so happy together. *Happy.* God, I want to feel it again, how I felt in this photo. "Maybe he's still in love with her, and that's why he hid it."

"That doesn't explain why he won't tell you about her," she points out. "Or why you lived with her for three years before she gave you up."

My lungs ache as I struggle to get air. "Maybe she died. Maybe he took me in because she died, and he keeps this photo because he wants to hold on to her memory."

"That's deep, Isa." She thrums her fingernails on top of the wheel, frowning. "Maybe a little too deep for your dad."

"Who knows how deep my dad is?" Tears prickle in the corners of my eyes. "I don't know him."

"No one really does when you think about it. He's practically secluded himself from the entire family."

She's right. No one really knows my dad, except for maybe Lynn, who practically controls his every move. I wonder if, at one time, my mom knew him. Like, *really* knew him. Were they happy? How did they end up together? Did she make him laugh? Did he make her smile? Was he the one who took the picture? Did the three of us ever spend time together?

All questions I may never get the answers to.

I smash my lips together as I stare at the photo.

Who are you? Where did you go?

How do I find you?

I tuck the photo into my pocket, say good-bye to Indigo, and then climb out of the car. Kai doesn't get out right away, so I open the back door and give him a little shake. His eyelashes flutter open and he blinks at me, disoriented.

"We're home," I tell him softly.

He sticks out his hand and wiggles his fingers. "Help me up."

I grab his hand and tug on his arm.

He slides to the edge of the seat and ducks out, bumping his head on the way.

"Ow." He rubs his head, frowning. "The sad thing is, I didn't even feel it."

"Then why'd you say *ow* for?" I tease as I give Indigo another wave and close the door.

She backs away, her headlights vanishing as she turns onto the road.

"Because it seemed necessary," Kai replies, belatedly answering my question. He hikes down the driveway, weaving back and forth.

Concerned he's not going to make it, I hurry after him as he heads for the sidewalk. Right at the last second, he skips to the side and bounds over the fence, clipping his boot on the top bar. His knees bang the fence, and then he lands on the other side on his back.

"Shit." I rush over to him and swing my leg over the fence.

I must be drunker than I thought, because climbing over is a lot more complicated than it should be. But I manage without falling then rush to Kai's side, kneeling in the grass beside him.

His eyes are closed, and he's lying still with his arm draped over his waist.

"Are you okay?" I ask, then panic when he doesn't respond. I lean over him and cup his scruffy cheek, trying to remember if he hit his head. "Kai, can you hear me?"

"No, I think you need to lean a little bit closer," he whispers. Then his eyes pop open, and a lazy half-grin spreads across his face. "Hey."

"Hey." I exhale, relaxing. "You scared me."

"It was just a little fall."

"Did you hit your head?"

"I don't think so." His nose twitches as strands of my hair tickle his face. "Your hair smells good. Like cookies."

"I'm surprised it doesn't smell like beer and sweat." I start to move back, but he combs his fingers through my hair and draws me closer.

"No, don't go," he whispers, his fingers finding my cheek.

I realize a second too late what he wants to do, and the lag in my thought process gives his lips just enough time to reach mine.

I gasp against his mouth as he urges my lips apart with his tongue. Warmth pulls through my veins, steals the air from my lungs, and sends explosions of heat throughout my body.

Holy hell almighty.

Right as I kiss him back, headlights shine across us as a car pulls into his driveway.

I trip to my feet and scoot back from him as reality sets in.

Oh. My. God. I just kissed Kai.

Kai sighs, pushing onto his elbows. "Well, this is going to suck."

At first, I think he's referring to the kiss. Then, as he gets to his feet, he mutters, "Isa, I'm so sorry you have to see this." He places himself in front of me, as if he's protecting me from something.

Before I can ask, the headlights turn off, and I peek

over his shoulder as I hear the doors slam. The only light around is from a few street and porch lights and the moon shining in the sky above us. I can barely make out his parents' silhouettes, though I can feel the tension in the air.

"What the hell are you doing out here?" Kai's dad asks as he stares him down with his arms crossed.

"I just got back," Kai says, sounding unsure of himself, so unlike the Kai I know.

"Do you realize how late it is?" his mother asks. "No, I don't even want to hear you try to lie your way out of this. Of course you know how late it is. But just like always, you don't care if you worry us."

"You were looking for me?" Kai asks, surprised.

"No. We were at an event," his mother replies curtly. "What if we had been looking for you? Imagine how worried we would've been."

"Yeah, I don't think you would've been that concerned." Kai yawns then shakes his head, getting sleepy again.

"Are you drunk?" his mother huffs, tapping her foot against the concrete.

"I'm sorry." Kai doesn't even try to lie his way out of it.

"Dammit, Kai. How many times have I told you, if you're going to act like a loser, then don't come home?" his dad snaps. "Why do you have to be such a fuck-up? Kyler never put us through this shit. Why can't you be more like him, instead of such a fucking loser all the time? Why don't you try making our lives simple, instead of so damn hard all the time? Fuck!" His dad kicks the tire.

"Because then we wouldn't get to have these little chats of ours," Kai mumbles under his breath.

"Get your damn ass in the house," his dad growls as he points at the door. "Right now, before I make you."

Sighing, Kai gives me a little push back toward the fence before he walks toward the house with his shoulders hunched. I slink into the shadows, wondering what will happen if they see me. Luckily, they seem too distracted by Kai.

His dad scolds him the entire way to the back steps then slaps him upside the back of his head as they disappear inside.

Poor Kai. I feel so bad for him. He sounded so beaten down, like he heard the same speech a million times. It reminds me so much of the way I react to situations.

I know how terrible he's probably feeling right now, and I want to go knock on the door and give him a hug, but know it'll probably just upset his parents more.

I make a promise to myself that, even if things are awkward tomorrow, which I'm guessing after the kiss they will be, that I'll give him that hug or something.

CHAPTER SIX

I DRANK MORE THAN I THOUGHT LAST NIGHT AND END UP spending almost the entire next day in bed. I keep having the same dream, where someone sneaks into my room while I'm sleeping and stares down at me in my bed, holding a paintbrush. Around six o'clock or so, I wake up and realize where the dream came from.

The second I open my eyes and fully come out of dreamland, my nostrils are assaulted by paint fumes. I sit up, look around for where the smell is coming from, and then smile.

A partially finished mural is painted on the wall opposite my bed. The colors are bright, forming a city, yet the shadows and fine lines give it a darker, gothic vibe.

Painted in front of the industrial scene is a girl who resembles one of the superheroes in my sketches. She's wearing a cape with her hands on her hips and a look in her eyes that reads: *I'm about to kick your ass.*

I roll out of bed, grab my leather jacket from the floor, and dig out my phone. I have one new message, and tensing, I open it.

T: U better pay up soon or u r going to get fucked up. Don't make me remind u what we did to DG.

I reread the message again then realize I have Kai's phone. I have no clue how I ended up with his.

I pick up my jacket again and fumble through my pockets until I find my phone. They look almost identical.

I set his phone on the nightstand and plug mine in since the battery is dead.

What I read in Kai's message haunts my thoughts as my phone boots up. Who's T? And why is he threatening Kai? And what the hell did he do to this DG guy? It has me really worried about him and what he's done to piss off people who are sketchy enough to threaten him.

Once I get my phone on, I plant my ass down on my bed and send Indigo a message.

Me: I can't believe u did all of that while I was sleeping. It's beautiful. Thanks so much!

Indigo: U R welcome! After last night, I thought u could use some cheering up.

Me: I totally could :) U r the best.

Indigo: I know. And FYI, u sleep like a rock. Seriously, I thought the fumes would wake u up, but nope.

Me: I was really hungover.

Indigo: I figured as much. Speaking of hangovers, how's your cute friend doing?

Me: I'm guessing u mean Kai.

Indigo: He's such a sweetie, Isa. Screw this Kyler dude. U should totally b going out with Kai.

Me: U haven't even met Kyler, so how can u say that?

Indigo: I don't have to meet Kyler. The way u and Kai were together was enough.

Me: I'm not going for either brother.

Indigo: Liar. U still have your sights set on Kyler. I can tell.

Me: He did ask me to go to his game yesterday.

I get hyped up and excited just thinking about it.

Indigo: Holy shit! Why didn't u text me?

Me: I got sidetracked with Kai and the party, but I was gonna tell u.

Indigo: Got distracted with Kai and the party. Interesting ...

Me: And on that note, I have to go.

Indigo: Liar! U r just running from the truth about u and Kai!

Me: There's no truth to me and Kai, because there's no me and Kai. We r just FRIENDS!

Indigo: That's how all true loves start.

Me: TTYL, matchmaker. I have to go take care of some stuff.

I put down my phone, feeling flustered over all the stuff she said. Kai may be cute and charming—and yeah, we shared that drunken kiss last night that made my body tingle in ways I don't understand—but I've never thought of him in the way Indigo was implying until she implied it. Now my mind is all overloaded with thoughts of me and Kai doing more than just kissing. It makes me really confused about myself, what I want, and what the hell I'm doing.

"Dammit, Indigo." I climb out of bed, grab a black shirt, a white skirt, and my gladiator sandals, and then head to the bathroom to take a shower and hopefully clear my mind.

By the time I'm all showered and cleaned up, I feel much better. But as I make it downstairs, my good mood goes *kerplunk*.

Hannah is in the kitchen, and she's not alone. With her are Val, one of her friends from high school, and a beefy guy I've never met before.

"Oh, look, it's Isabella Smellera," Hannah sneers as she slams the fridge door.

Val giggles as she collects a plastic cup from off the countertop. "Nice one, Hannah."

"You know that nickname doesn't bother me anymore," I say to her as I cross the kitchen and head for the back door

"Keep telling yourself that." Hannah removes the plastic off a vegetable tray and opens a cup of ranch dip.

I note all the alcohol bottles on the kitchen table and the shiny pink shoes and glittery black dress she's wearing. "Are you having a party?"

"Yep. Sure am. And you're not invited." Hannah readjusts her boobs, and Beefy Dude grins as he watches. "So you better find someplace else to sleep."

"You can't kick me out of my own house," I say, grabbing the doorknob.

"I can't, huh? How about I just text Mom and Dad and find out how they feel?" She laughs snidely when I remain silent. "Yeah, that's what I thought. So get your shit and get out of here."

I fight every damn urge in my body to go back and ninja kick the crap out of her.

Don't let her get to you. Just walk away, Isa.

I yank open the door and step outside, her laughter hitting my back, shoving all thoughts of Hannah aside as I head over to the Meyers' to return Kai's phone to him.

As I hike up the driveway, Indigo's texts ring through my head and nerves bubble in my stomach.

"You don't like Kai like that," I mutter to myself as I march up the porch stairs to the back door. "You're just friends. You're just friends." I knock on the door, and when it swings open, Kyler is standing in the doorway.

He's wearing dark jeans and a red T-shirt that brings out the color in his eyes. His hair is all crazy, like he's been stressed out and pulling on the roots. He looks so sexy right now that I can't stop ogling him.

"Hey, Isa." He places his hand on his head and flattens down the crazy hair.

Hearing him say my name makes my heart thud deafeningly inside my chest, and blood roars in my eardrums at the sight of him.

"Is Kai here?" I want to jump up and down that my voice came out steady.

"You actually just missed him." He braces his palms on the doorframe, and I try not to gawk at his flexed arm muscles. "What'd you need him for? Maybe I can help."

My fingers tremble slightly as I stuff my hand into my jacket pocket and grab Kai's phone. "I'm not sure how it happened, but somehow during the mass confusion that was last night, I ended up with his phone."

He takes the phone from me, his forehead creasing. "You guys hung out last night?"

"Yeah, we went to a party one of his friends had." *And then kissed in the driveway.*

He glances up from the phone, his confusion deepening. "You went to one of his friends' parties?" he asks, and I nod, puzzled because ... well, he's puzzled. "Isa, I don't want you to take this the wrong way, but I don't think you should hang out with Kai's friends. They'll get you in trouble."

I don't know whether I'm touched that he's looking out for me or annoyed that he thinks I'm too naive to take care of myself.

"It was just one party. I don't really hang out with them."

"Okay, it's just that …" He massages the back of his neck. "You've never really hung out with Kai up until recently, so I just wanted to warn you that he hasn't been making the best choices lately."

"Thanks for the warning." I start back down the stairs, surprisingly relieved to be getting away from the uncomfortable conversation.

"Hey, what are you doing for the next couple of hours?" he asks before I can make my escape.

I stop on the bottom step and turn around. "I was actually going to head home and blog for a little while. Then I probably have to find a way to get over to my grandma's, so I can crash there for the night."

"How come you need a place to crash?" he asks, glancing over at my house.

"Hannah's having a party, and I'm not allowed there while she has one." I shrug, wondering if he's going to act all offish now since I brought up Hannah.

He pats the doorframe a couple of times. "If you want to wait for me to get done baking, I can give you a ride."

"Really?" Tap dances and fist pumps all around. "That'd actually be super great."

Face-palm. Seriously? What the hell is with all the "supers" every time I'm around him?

He motions for me to come inside as he steps back into the washroom.

I jog up the steps, squeeze by him into the house, and take a whiff of the air. "What are you baking?"

He shuts the door then moves past me and into the kitchen. "Chocolate chip cookies." When I start to grin, he adds, "Don't get too excited. I've never done this before, so I'm not sure how they're going to turn out." He stops in front of the island that's covered with bowls, spoons, eggshells, and layers of flour. "Maybe you could help me out. I know how much you like sweet stuff. Every time you used to come over here, you always ate all the cookies."

I'm surprised he remembers that.

"I don't think I'll be any help," I tell him apologetically. "I like to eat them, not bake them."

He picks up a spoon and looks over a page of a cookbook. "I'm sure the two of us can figure it out if we put our heads together."

"Okay, we can try that." I stand beside him, recollecting all the times Lynn baked cookies and how she did it. Since she never let me help her, though, I lack great knowledge on baking. "Where are you in the recipe?"

"I'm not sure." He licks batter off the spoon then gags. "God, that's disgusting."

"That's because you basically just ate eggs and flour." I peer into one of the mixing bowls then cover my mouth, trying not to laugh at the bubbling goo inside.

"Is it that bad?" he asks, setting the spoon down.

I shake my head, laughter choking me to death. "I'm sorry. I know I shouldn't laugh."

"No, you really should." He laughs with me. "This is such a disaster."

I get my laughter under control. "Why are you even trying to bake?"

"It's for my mom. She does this fundraiser bake sale every year for the school, and she always takes on too much, so I usually help her out." He pulls a face at the mess on the counter. "Usually, she supervises."

"Disaster or not, it was really nice of you to try."

"Yeah, I just hope she has time to fix the mess." He picks up the bowl and puts it in the sink, giving up.

I get an idea right as he starts to clean up.

"I might know someone who can help us."

"Really?" He perks up as he turns on the sink to rinse the bowl out. "Who?"

"My grandma. She's not the greatest cook, but she can make a mean batch of cookies."

"You think she'd help?"

"I can text her and find out." I slide my phone out of my pocket. "I need to tell her I'm spending the night there, anyway."

"Thanks, Isa." His lips tip up into an adorable half-grin. "That's really awesome of you."

"It's not a big deal." I'm such a liar. It's such a big deal to me that my hands shake as I text Grandma Stephy.

Me: Hey, can I stay the night there? Hannah kicked me out.

"It is a big deal," Kyler insists. "You're always so nice and always willing to help people, even when they haven't treated you as nicely as they should."

My brows furrow. "Are you talking about you?"

He nods, cleaning a glob of yolk off the counter with a paper towel. "I haven't always treated you as nicely as I should. I never even thanked you for making my free throw skills awesome."

I shrug. "Like I said, it's not—"

"Don't say it isn't a big deal," he cuts me off. "I've been thinking about this a lot lately, mainly when things with your sister went south, and I realized I can come off as an arrogant dick sometimes."

"Why did things going south with my sister make you realize that?" I don't know why I ask. I just have this overwhelming urge to know.

"I kissed her," he says almost guiltily. "And I never should've because I didn't like her that way. But the fact of the matter is I kissed her, she took it the wrong way, and it made me feel like such a douche. And then I started thinking about how many times I acted like a douche, and it started to drive me crazy."

"Hannah's ego can take it. I promise."

"I know." He steadily carries my gaze. "But there are other people who might—who shouldn't have to put up with my shit."

I shrug. "You never really did anything to me. And you've always stuck up for me when other people were acting like douches."

"Yeah, I guess." He tosses the paper towel into the trash then scratches his forehead. "You know, you're so easy to talk to. I don't know how, but I somehow forgot you were like that."

"You're not the only guy who's told me that."

"Really?" He seems intrigued. "I guess I'll have to think of a better compliment then."

"I guess you will." The light, flirty tone of my voice shocks the crap out of me. I honestly feel kind of silly for even attempting to flirt.

Fortunately, my phone buzzes.

"Hold on a sec," I tell Kyler. "My grandma just texted me back."

Grandma Stephy: Goddamn that child. She's such a pain in the ass. Of course u can stay, but does your father know about this?

Me: We should just keep this between us. If I text him about Hannah kicking me out, it's just going to start more drama, and there's way too much of that already.

Grandma Stephy: Okay, sweetie. I'll come pick u up.

Me: I actually have a ride. I need to ask u for another favor. I have a friend who has a baking crisis and needs help making a few batches of chocolate chip

cookies. I love eating me some cookies, but u know I suck at actually making them, so I thought maybe u could help us out?

Grandma Stephy: So, u want me to bake for u? Jesus, aren't u needy? ;)

Me: I know. It's your fault, though, for giving me everything I want. ;)

Grandma Stephy: Glad to c u haven't lost your sense of humor.

Me: That'll never happen, no matter how bad things get.

Grandma Stephy: You're a strong girl, Isa. U really r. And I love u to death. I'll bake for u, but only if u tell me who this friend is.

Me: Um ... Kyler Meyers, a guy who lives next-door to me.

Grandma Stephy: Is that the boy u and Indigo were always whispering about?

Me: Maybe

Grandma Stephy: Interesting.

Me: Please don't say anything weird while we're there.

Grandma Stephy: I'll try my best, but no promises.

"So, what'd she say?" Kyler asks. "Will she help us out?"

I glance from the screen to find him standing in front of me, close enough I can smell his cologne. "She said she's down."

"Really? That's so fucking awesome. Thanks, Isa." He hugs me. Actually freaking hugs me, with both arms and everything. "I owe you big time. And not just for the cookies, but for teaching me how to kick ass at free throws, too."

"I am pretty awesome," I joke, daring to wrap an arm around him and hug him back.

"You're more than awesome. You're like the awesomest of awesomeness."

I smile at his sentence. It sounds like something I would say.

"Okay, who died?" Kai says, sounding like he's right next to us.

"Huh?" Kyler pulls away from me, and his gaze cuts to his brother. "What are you talking about? No one died."

He might be wrong. I'm pretty sure my heart stopped beating for a second or two there.

Kai gives me a condemning look as he drops his jacket onto the table. "I don't know. Isa might have."

My lips do a great Elvis impression as Kai and I stare each other down. Surprisingly, Kai is the one to give in first and whisks by me to grab a package of Oreos from the cupboard.

"Well, it looks like you two are having a fan-fucking-tastic time," Kai says dryly. "I'll leave you guys to your awkward hugging."

"I actually came here to bring you your phone," I call

out after him as he turns to leave the room. "I somehow ended up with it last night."

He turns around, facing me again. "I was wondering where that went. I was worried I lost it at Bradon's, and he'd already hocked it."

I notice a red mark on the side of his cheek and wonder if it's from where his dad slapped him upside the head last night.

You need to make sure everything's okay.

"He sounds like a great friend," Kyler remarks as he puts the eggs back into the fridge.

"Yep, the best," Kai quips, peeling apart an Oreo to lick off the frosting. Then he fixes his eyes on me. "Did you bring my phone with you? I've been expecting a few texts."

Kyler chucks it at him before I can answer.

Luckily, Kai has the reflexes of a ninja and effortlessly catches it. "Thanks." He smiles at Kyler, but it's not friendly. "Have fun with your new friend, Isa." He winks at me, trying to get under my skin, then turns to leave, scrolling through his messages.

I hurry after him as he walks toward the stairway. "Who's this T guy?"

He glances down at me, not looking very happy. "You know who he is. He's the dude who talked to us last night."

"But who is he exactly?"

"Just some dude."

"Don't lie to me, Kai. I read one of your messages from him." I shift my weight as he glares at me. "It wasn't on purpose. I thought it was my phone."

"You should probably just forget what you read." He punches a few buttons then stuffs his phone into the back pocket of his worn jeans.

"Are you in trouble?" I ask. "Because that message … it sounds like you're in trouble."

"I'm always in trouble," he replies simply then stuffs a cookie into his mouth and licks his lips.

His tongue.

Those lips.

That kiss.

"Kai, about last night and what happened in the driveway—"

"Relax," he cuts me off. "I kiss almost everyone when I'm drunk."

"I wasn't actually going to say anything about the kiss, but thanks for the info on your kissing routine," I say, and he stares at me, unimpressed. "I just want to make sure you're okay … with what happened with your dad." I suck in an inhale, mustering up the courage. "And to give you this." I wrap my arms around him and give him a quick hug that lasts just long enough for me to notice he smells like vanilla frosting. "You looked like you needed this last night, but I didn't want to make your parents madder, so I thought I'd wait until today."

The hug is not as awkward as I thought it would be,

but when I step back, Kai's staring at me with his mouth hanging open.

"You're a strange girl sometimes." He grabs another cookie from the package with a quizzical look on his face. "But in the best way possible."

"So I've been told," I say with a small smile. "You're okay, though, right?"

He nods, swallowing hard. "I'm okay."

I glance at the welt on his cheek. "Promise?"

His fingers drift to his cheek, and he winces. "I promise." Then he turns his back on me and jogs up the stairs without saying anything else.

I'm not positive I believe he's okay, but I'm not sure what else to do, other than keeping an eye on him.

I head back to the kitchen, feeling sullen.

Kyler has everything cleaned up by the time I walk in, and he has his jacket and shoes on, ready to go.

"Everything okay?" he asks as he collects the car keys from the counter.

I nod. "Yeah, everything's fine."

That's the second time I've lied in the last ten minutes. Who I'm lying to, I'm not quite sure.

CHAPTER SEVEN

BY THE TIME WE ARRIVE AT MY GRANDMA STEPHY'S
house, she's halfway done baking the cookies. I give her
a good, stern lecture for not waiting for us, and she tells
me that she doesn't need my sucky baking skills tainting
her cookies and to go sit my ass down in the living
room while she works her Baker Fairy Magic in the
kitchen.

"She's funny," Kyler says after we settle on the living
room sofa.

"Yeah, she's pretty funny, I guess." I shift on the sofa,
feeling nervous as hell with how close he's sitting next
to me.

"You smile around her a lot," he remarks as he slides
his arm across the back of the sofa.

"Do I not smile a lot when I'm not around her?" *You
notice that I don't?*

"I've seen you smile a couple of times," he says. "But not a lot."

"Maybe it's because you haven't been around me a lot," I reply with a shrug. "Generally, I try to be a happy person, even when things are super sucky. And I'm seriously easy to please. I mean, give me a cookie and a comic book, and I'm like a freaking unicorn sniffing rainbows."

"*A unicorn sniffing a rainbow?*" He cocks a brow.

I shrug, picking at my nails. "What? Unicorns are totally crazy happy when they sniff rainbows."

He chuckles. "Funny. I didn't know unicorns were real or that they sniffed rainbows."

"Oh, they're totally real." I grin. "Now, I'm not positive the rainbow part is true, but I like to think it is because I'm just that awesome."

"That you are." He gently tugs on a strand of my hair for God knows what reason. "You remember that time you wore a cape to school?"

I pull a face. "Yeah, I remember. Don't judge me, though. I was, like, ten and going through this phase where I wanted to be a witch."

"No, I wasn't judging you at all," he quickly says. "I always thought it was cool you were so comfortable with being yourself." I glance down at my stylish outfit, and he hurriedly adds, "I like this look, too. I promise. And you're still you and everything. And really cool and comfortable with yourself." He's rambling and sounds nervous, and I can barely keep up with what he's saying. He finally takes a breath and shakes his head at himself. "I don't know what my problem is. You've totally thrown me off my game."

He's trying to use his game on me?

He moves his arm from the back of the sofa and rakes his fingers through his hair. "You just make me nervous."

I almost bust up laughing. *I'm* making Kyler nervous?

"Are you being serious?"

He nods, lowering his hand to his lap. "I'm usually better at reading people, but with you ... I have no idea what you're thinking." He waits, like he expects me to tell him.

I shake my head. "There is no way I'm telling you what goes on in here." I tap my temple. "If I did, you might run out the door."

"I doubt that." He sits up straight and twists to face me. "How about we try it and see? You tell me one thing you're thinking, and we'll see if it scares me enough that I run."

"That seems like a game I'll lose no matter what because, either you leave, or you stay here and think I'm crazy."

"Okay, well, how about this? You just tell me one thing, and I won't think you're crazy and I'll stay."

"How can you possibly predict that?" I ask, amused. "Are you secretly a psychic?"

"I have an aunt who is," he says in all seriousness.

"Really? That's crazy cool. Does she, like, tell you your fortunes and everything? Do you know when you're going to die?"

He shakes his head. "Nope. I'm not telling you anything more until you tell me something about you."

I give an overdramatic sigh. "Fine, but don't say I didn't warn you." I press my lips together, thinking, *What could I possibly tell him about me that won't make him think I'm crazy?* All my interests are weird, and I don't think he'd get my obsession with zombies. Maybe I could tell him some of the things I did this summer, like dancing at the club or kissing Nyle ...

Oh, my God, why would I tell him that?

"I skinny-dipped in a pool this summer." I slap my hand over my mouth.

Holy shit. Out of all the things, that's what I decided to go with?

"You did what?" From the kitchen, Grandma Stephy stares at me in shock.

"We weren't totally naked," I tell her, mentally cursing myself. I'd been doing so well, lightly flirting, saying fun things, and then my weirdo gene decided to make a grand appearance.

She points the spoon she's holding at me. "We'll talk about this later." She goes back to her baking, leaving me to sit here in shame as I blush.

"You really did that?" Kyler asks, trying not to smile.

"I didn't mean to say that aloud. I do stuff like that

sometimes—talk without thinking." I lean back on the sofa. "But yeah, Indigo—my cousin—and I went swimming in our underwear when we were in Scotland. It was more her idea than mine. She was really big on making sure we had a ton of crazy experiences."

"It sounds like that's exactly what you did." He playfully bumps knees with mine. "Maybe one day you can tell me more crazy stuff you did."

I bite back a smile. "Maybe one day, if you're lucky."

He grins, totally noting my flirty tone. "Maybe when you come watch my game, we can go out and get something to eat. Hit up a party or something."

Okay, he's definitely asking me out.

I get all giddy then hesitate. I don't know why, but at that moment, I think about Kai and the party we went to. We had so much fun. More fun than I've ever had. Would I have that much fun with Kyler? I'll never know unless I go. Besides, going out with Kyler has been my dream since practically forever. I owe it to my eight-year-old self to do this. And talking with him today has been so easy.

"That sounds like fun," I say. "And I think it has crazy adventure potential."

"I think so, too." He glances at his watch. "You'll have to be the leader of our little adventure. I'm not very good at impulsive things."

"I'll think of something," I promise as he glances at his watch again.

Am I boring him to death?

"I still can't believe you went to Scotland," he says, looking back at me in awe. "I mean, I knew you went somewhere for the summer, but not Scotland."

I wonder where he thought I was this summer. Did he buy into Hannah's mental institution thing?

"Where exactly did you think I went this summer? I'm just curious."

"I knew you went on a trip with your grandma, but Kai never said exactly where you went." He pauses, seeming conflicted. "Were you worried about Hannah's rumor about the mental institution thing? Because you should know, no one believes that."

"Really?" I hug a pillow against my chest. "Why not?"

"Kai told everyone that it wasn't true." He intently studies my expression. "You didn't know that?"

"No, I didn't. He never said anything to me about it." My thoughts drift back to Kai.

Why didn't he tell me? I wish I knew so that I could have at least thanked him.

God, I need to thank him, like, a lot.

"Okay, I'm new at this not-being-a-douche thing, so you can totally tell me if I'm being rude," he says with a hint of remorse in his voice. "But the games on in, like, five minutes, and I—"

I laugh, cutting him off. "Kyler, you can turn on the game. It's cool."

"Are you sure?"

"Yep." I'm just glad I know what all the watch-checking was about.

I turn on the television for him, and his attention instantly goes right to the screen.

I think about sending Kai a text to thank him, but a text doesn't feel like the right way.

No, it should be in person.

Eventually, the air permeates with the scent of soon-to-be-done, yummy-in-my-tummy cookies. I've just started contemplating getting up and going into the kitchen, wondering if it makes me rude, when Kyler turns to me as a commercial comes on.

"You want me to explain the rules to you?" he asks. "If you're going to come watch me play, you should probably know what's going on. That way, you can cheer me on when I kick some ass." He winks. "I kick ass a lot."

"I bet you do," I tell him, smiling from the wink. "You can try to explain the rules to me, but I'm going to warn you that I usually don't catch on to stuff very quickly, unless I'm actually doing it."

"I guess we'll have to throw the ball around sometime, then." The dimpled grin appears again, and my pulse quickens. "But I'll try to explain it now, if that's cool." He gets an excited look in his eyes, like he's pumped to be doing this.

The look is contagious and gets me pumped, too, even if we're going to be talking about football.

He faces the television again, sitting back on the sofa

and putting his arm on the back again. "Okay, so how much do you know about football?"

"A little bit." I'm hyperaware that he's playing with my hair. I don't even think he realizes he's doing it. "My dad watches it sometimes, but he's not a fan of me being anywhere near him when he does."

"But you're good at sports, right?"

"I'm okay, I guess. Football's always seemed kind of boring to me, though." I offer him an apologetic look. "Sorry."

"It's okay. I'm not one of those guys who thinks the game is everything. You don't have to like it. I just want to try to get you to kind of maybe like it enough not to be bored out of your mind when you're at my game, okay?"

I nod, and he smiles, jumping right in, yammering about downs, defense and offense, goals, two-point conversions. By the time he slows down, my mind is on football overdrive.

"It's okay if you don't get it all at first," he says when he notes the crazed, wild-eyed look I'm probably rocking.

"Good, because I'm definitely not getting it at all." I look at the television screen. "I mean, I get the gist of it, but there are so many rules and so many guys just running around on a field."

"I'm probably boring you to death, aren't I?" He shifts positions, sitting up straight and lowering his hand to his lap. "I have an idea. How about for every rule I tell you,

you get to tell me one thing about comics and superheroes?"

"You know I'm into that stuff?"

He nods. "I've seen some of your drawings at school. They're pretty good."

I mull over his offer. "All right, Kyler, you have yourself a deal."

AN HOUR LATER, HE'S LEAVING WITH HIS FRESHLY BAKED cookies, his head crammed full of superpower knowledge. I feel like I'm floating on clouds and skipping on rainbows, even if my head aches from football facts.

The second the door closes, I overdramatically fall to the floor.

"What the hell just happened?" I say, draping my arm over my head. "Did I seriously just spend over an hour talking to Kyler about football and Jedi mind skills?"

Grandma Stephy laughs at me as she starts piling dirty bowls into the sink. "To be young and in love again. I've completely forgotten how silly love can make someone."

"I'm not in love with Kyler. I'm just ..." I push up on my elbows. "You did hear him, right? I mean, I didn't dream what just happened, did I? Because I've dreamed about him asking me out for a long, long time." Well, up until recently. Lately, my dreams have been chock-full of worries about never finding my mom.

"You're awake, I promise." She grabs a dishtowel and tosses it at my face. "Now, get your ass over here and help me clean up this mess."

I drag myself off the floor and put the flour and sugar in the pantry.

"Can I ask you a question?"

"Isabella Anders, you need to stop asking that question before you ask a question," she gripes as she puts the egg carton back into the fridge.

"Sorry, but I kind of wanted to prepare you for what I was about to ask."

She pauses, worry creasing her face. "What is it?"

I sigh then tell her about the photo and the birth certificate, omitting the details of what Kai and I did with the certificate. I also tell her about the texts I've been receiving.

"I thought I told you to leave this alone and let me handle it? That snooping around wasn't a good idea," she says when I'm finished.

"I can't just sit around and wonder what's going on." I pull out a barstool and sit down. "Besides, I'm not even the one who found the certificate."

"Yeah, I think that part of your story's really strange. I don't understand why someone would just leave it on your bed." Her puzzlement turns into a scowl. "I really wish you would've told me about these texts earlier."

"Why? It only would've just worried you. And if it is Hannah, you can't stop her from sending them."

"But what if it isn't Hannah?" She swallows hard and shifts her gaze to the counter.

"Is there something else you aren't telling me?" I question her suddenly suspicious behavior.

She shakes her head, looks back and me, and forces a smile. "No. Not about this."

Way to be vague, Grandma.

I have no idea what she could be keeping from me, and I start to question if maybe I'm over-analyzing it. Maybe all the stress of everything is starting to wear on me

I rest my arms on the counter with a sigh. "This is driving me crazy not knowing what happened—where my mom is, who she is. I feel like I don't know who I am anymore. Like I'm just this person floating around in the world, lost, without a family. And I don't want to float anymore."

She takes a seat on a barstool beside me. "Honey, I know it's confusing right now. Just give me some time to get the story out of your father. I know it's not happening as fast as you like, but I really do believe that eventually he'll break down and tell us if I push him enough."

I glance down at my bandaged knee, remembering the last time she tried to push him. "You really think you'll be able to get him to tell you?"

She hesitantly nods. "Eventually, yes."

I want to believe her—I really do—but my dad seems pretty dead set on no one telling me anything about my mom.

"Do you have that photo on you?" she asks, wiping her hands off on a dishtowel.

I retrieve the picture from my pocket and hand it to her.

A faint smile rises on her lips. "You look a lot like her." She shakes her head, looking up at me. "I'm so sorry you have to go through this."

"It's not your fault." I suck back the tears, get up, and start sweeping the kitchen floor.

One question is stuck in my head. How did my dad manage to keep my mom such a secret?

"Isa, stop sweeping. The last thing you should be doing is cleaning." She stands up and grabs her purse from the table. "Why don't we go out for dinner? We can go to that diner you love, and I'll even let you order dessert first."

"That sounds nice." I smile so she'll relax. Deep down, though, I know that even sugar isn't going to cure the hole forming in the center of my heart.

The only thing that will ever fix it is finding my real mom.

CHAPTER EIGHT

SHIT HAS OFFICIALLY HIT THE FAN. SUNDAY MORNING, when I return home from my grandma's, Lynn is there. And she's alone.

"Where's Dad?" I ask as I enter the kitchen, which is still trashed from Hannah's party.

"He had to make a quick trip out to Florida for work," she answers, sorting through the stack of mail on the counter littered with beer cans and plastic cups.

"How long will he be gone?" My muscles ravel into knots as I remember how shitty she treated me the last time my dad went on a business trip.

"A week or so." She sets the mail down and gives me a look that sends a chill down my spine. "And I'm under strict orders to make sure you do your chores while he's gone."

"My room and bathroom are already clean," I say, hoping Hannah's friends didn't trash those rooms, too.

"That's nice, but I was talking about your new, extra chores." Her smile grows as her gaze sweeps around the kitchen.

"I didn't make this mess," I say, fighting to keep calm. Losing my cool is only going to make this worse. "I wasn't even here."

"How do I know that for sure?" She grabs the handle of her suitcase and drags it with her as she heads for the door. "It makes much more sense to me that you would have the party. Hannah's too good of a girl. Now hurry and get this place cleaned so I can give you your list of chores."

I grip the edge of the counter and bite back a stream of expletives clawing up my throat.

This is going to be a hellishly long week.

FOR THE NEXT WEEK AND A HALF, I PLAY THE ROLE OF Isabella Smellera, cleaning and taking on the role as the maid for Lynn and Hannah.

I thought my dad would be back by now. Every time I ask Lynn about when he's coming home, she just shrugs and says, "He'll be back when he gets back. Now get to work."

I try to call my dad a couple of times, but my calls go

straight to voicemail. I try texts and emails, receiving no reply.

By the time Friday rolls around, it's been two weeks since I've seen or heard from my father, and I'm beginning to get really concerned that maybe Lynn murdered him on their getaway and dropped his body into the ocean.

"I'm sure he's fine," Kai says when I express my concern to him during third period. "I know Lynn's a bitch and everything, but I don't think she'd kill anyone." He flashes me a teasing grin, trying to lighten the mood. "It'd be too messy for her, and she wouldn't risk getting blood on her clothes."

"I hope you're right." I add shading to the drawing I'm working on, instead of doing the math assignment.

Kai and I haven't really hung out very much lately, mostly because I've been too busy cleaning the house and cooking for Lynn and Hannah. Same with me and Kyler, though we do have a date scheduled for tomorrow. Now, whether I can get out of the house to actually go on it is an entirely different question.

As for Kai and his issues with his parents, I haven't had a chance to ask him more about that. I haven't noticed any more welts on him or heard any yelling next-door. That doesn't mean I'm going to stop keeping an eye on him.

And the kiss … well, somehow the two of us have

silently agreed never to mention it again. I think about it sometimes, though. Just like I think about Kyler.

I'm a very, very confused girl.

"I'm always right," Kai jokes, reaching across the row to flick my hair with a pencil. "You should know that by now."

"Kai and Isa, keep it down," Mr. Marelli warns from his desk.

Half the class turns to stare at us. While the staring has toned down, besides this instance, I still haven't made any real friends. I do have a few people I chat with during classes, thanks to Kai and that party when he introduced me to people.

Kai rolls his eyes, but faces forward in his desk again and starts scribbling the answers on the assignment sheet.

I work on my sketch again, getting lost as I draw the superhero version of me.

"You need a sidekick," Kai whispers, leaning over in his chair to look at my work.

"I usually have one," I whisper back as I draw an angled line. "But I thought I'd go solo on this mission."

"No way. I want to come." He does his pouty lip, fluttery eyelash move. "Come on; make me your sidekick."

Grinning, I press the pencil to the paper and give in to his request.

He smiles, relaxing back in his chair with his arms

tucked behind his head. "See? The move does work on you."

My grin grows as I finish the drawing then hold it up for him to see.

"Why does my head look so big?" he wonders, putting the tip of the pencil to his lip.

"It has to be big," I explain, "in order to fit your super-hero name."

"Which is?"

"Ego Man."

"Isa, come on," he whines. "I know you can do better than that."

"I don't know. Ego Man seems pretty fitting."

"Fine, but if I'm Ego Man, then you're Vain Girl, and our kryptonite is mirrors because we stare in them for too long."

I giggle softly. "I'm not vain."

"And I don't have an inflated ego," he insists. "But, hey, you're the one who wanted to play this game."

"A game I'm winning." I show him my pearly whites.

He rolls his eyes. "In your dreams."

"Isa and Kai, this is your final warning," Mr. Marelli warns, scowling at us.

We both grow quiet until Kai says, "Then what happens to us? I mean, his threat seemed so ominous, but he didn't finish it."

I choke on a laugh, and Kai grins. Unfortunately for

us, Mr. Marelli doesn't think it's so funny and makes Kai move to the desk at the front of the classroom.

I spend the rest of class working on the assignment and dreading lunch, since I still spend it sitting alone in the cafeteria.

When the bell rings, I slowly put my stuff away to kill time.

"What are you doing for lunch?" Kai asks as he strolls down the aisle toward my desk.

"What I always do." I swing my backpack over my shoulder. "Go to the cafeteria and eat lunch."

"Ew, you eat in the cafeteria?" He pulls an I'm-gonna-barf face.

"It's the only place to eat since I don't have a car to drive anywhere."

"I don't have my car today, either. I had to let Kyler borrow it because his is in the shop." He frowns as if just realizing this.

"You can always eat with me," I offer. "In the ewie cafeteria."

His expression contorts with disgust. "There's no way I'm eating that food." He looks at the clock then at the door. "Come on; I have an idea."

I follow him out into the busy hallway where he finds a girl named Marla, who I think's a junior and who has a car. Using his eyelash fluttering move, he sweet-talks her into giving us a ride to Sunnyvale Burger Drive-In, although she doesn't seem too thrilled I'm included in the "us."

I spend most of the drive in the backseat, listening to her laugh at everything Kai says, even stuff that's not funny at all. When we reach the burger place, Kai thanks her for the ride then hops out and opens the door for me.

"Wait? You don't need a ride back to school?" she asks, leaning over the console and smiling at him as her cleavage pops out of her top. "Because I don't mind giving you one."

"We're actually going to walk somewhere after we get our food." Kai shuts the door after I climb out.

The hope in her eyes goes *poof*, and I kind of feel bad for her.

"Okay, well, if you ever need a ride again, just let me know." With that, she glares at me before pushing the shifter into reverse and backing out of the space.

"I think I'm cramping your style," I tell Kai as we head for the entrance doors. "Did you see the dirty look she gave me?"

Kai feigns dumb. "I didn't notice anything."

"You liar." I pinch his ribs.

He laughs as he opens the door and lets me walk through first. "You're so violent all the time."

"Just admit it," I say as I walk up to the counter. "You totally just played her."

"I told her straight up that we needed a ride." He examines the menu above the register. "She knew the plan the entire time—that I was going to get lunch with you. She let herself get played."

I decide to let it go because I'm dying to ask something else.

"Why *are* you eating lunch with me? You never have before."

"Usually, I have stuff to do at lunch." He keeps his attention fixed on the menu. "But since I don't have a car today, that stuff's been put on hold until tomorrow."

"What kind of stuff?"

"Just stuff."

Ever since I read the text from T, I've been really worried about him. I keep waiting for him to show up at school with bruises or broken bones, but so far, he seems okay. Still, I have to wonder what exactly he owes this T guy that would lead to such threats.

"But you're okay, right?"

"I'm always okay," he says without looking at me.

I don't think I believe him.

After we get our lunch, we leave the burger place and start down the sidewalk, not in the direction of our school.

"Where are we going?" I ask then sip on the straw of my shake.

He winks at me as he pops a fry into his mouth. "It's a surprise."

I pull my aviator sunglasses down over my eyes to

block out the blinding sunlight. "We won't be late for class, though, right?"

"We might be a few minutes late." He puts his own sunglasses on. "But I promise it'll be worth it."

He picks up his pace, and I chase after him as he makes a right and ducks into the park. The moment he jogs to the grassy area, I know where he's going, and it makes me grin like a goof.

I race after him as he sprints toward the hollowed out tree tucked away near the rickety old seesaw. When we reach it, Kai ducks in, and I follow.

Since we're taller than we used to be, getting us both in becomes a puzzle. We end up sitting side by side with our legs sticking out of the entrance.

"I miss coming here," I state as I peel the wrapper off my hamburger. "It's so quiet and peaceful."

"I'm actually surprised they haven't cut the tree down yet," he says, pulling his burger out of the bag. "They've cut down a ton of them already."

I pick off the pickles and take a bite of my burger. "Maybe this one's still here because they know it's magical."

Kai chuckles at me as he chews his food. "Maybe, but I doubt it."

"You never know." I steal a fry from him and pop it into my mouth. "It could be magical."

His expression tightens. "I don't believe in magic anymore, so I can't agree with you."

The edge in his tone makes my concern for his well-being go up about fifty thousand notches.

"Kai, I know you don't want to talk about it—you've made that pretty clear. Just promise me you're going to be okay. That the threat that T guy made to you won't really happen."

He stares out of the hole, chewing on his food. "I'll be okay."

"Promise?"

He looks at me, his eyes smoldering. "Isa, you don't need to worry about me. I can take care of myself."

"I know I don't *need* to worry about you," I say, sounding a little worked up. "But I do."

"Why?" he wonders, still keeping his intense stare fixed on me.

I swallow hard. "Because I just do."

I haven't thanked him yet for telling everyone that Hannah's rumor was false, and for everything else he's done for me.

"Kai, I want to thank you."

"Oh, yeah? For what?" He seems really distracted.

"For telling everyone I didn't spend the summer in a mental institution."

"You found out about that?"

I nod. "I've been meaning to thank you, but I wanted to make sure it was when we were alone so I could press how much it means to me. No one's ever done something like that for me, especially when I was such a dork."

"It's not a big deal." His gaze drops to my lips, and he wets his own lips with his tongue. "It's really not."

I'm not sure if he's talking to me or himself, but he seems extremely fascinated with my lips.

Holy shit, is he going to kiss me again?

Holy shit, do I want him to kiss me again?

And while we're both sober?

Sober equals no excuses. Sober means we both want it.

Before I can decide what I'm going to do, the seesaw outside lets out an ear-scratching squeak, and Kai and I both shudder.

"God, I think that just broke my eardrum." He presses his finger to his ear and works his jaw back and forth.

I free a trapped breath, relieved the noise happened so that it broke the intense moment. I honestly don't know what I would've done if Kai kissed me while we were sober. Part of me craves another taste of his soft lips again and the explosions I felt inside, while another part of me can't help thinking of Kyler, which means I shouldn't kiss Kai.

I need to figure out what I want.

"We should probably get going," Kai says, gathering our trash, "if we're going to get you back in time for class."

"Yeah, we probably should." I climb out of the tree, taking the rest of the trash with me.

The walk back to school is quiet. I want to break the

silence because it's driving me crazy and makes me kind of sad. Kai and I never have awkward silence. I don't know what to say to him, though, since I'm a little unclear on why he seems so standoffish. Was it because of the kiss? Or something else?

"So, I'm going to a party tomorrow," he says as we turn and head up the path that leads to the entrance doors of the school. "I was thinking, if you wanted to, you could come with me."

"That sounds fun, and I really wish I could go." I really mean it. I wish I could go with him. "But ... I already told Kyler I'd go to his game."

"Oh, okay." Kai looks as perplexed as I feel.

I pick at a loose thread on the bottom of my dress as awkward silence stretches between us again. I hate this. I want to go back to our playful conversations.

"Maybe if it gets over in time, I can meet up with you, though," I say.

"Yeah, maybe." His forehead creases as he pulls open the door. "Are you driving with him? Or are you meeting him there?"

"He said I could ride with him. Why?"

He shrugs as he holds the door open for me. "Just wondering if it's a date or not." He joins me in the hall-way, letting the door go. "Sounds like a date to me, if he's picking you up." He grows quiet as he takes out his phone, glances at the screen, and chews on his bottom lip. "I have to go. I'll see you later, okay?" With that, he strides off down the hallway.

I watch him until he disappears around the corner, and then I head for my locker, my mind swimming in a sea of confusion where nothing makes sense, not even myself, which is sadly becoming my motto in life.

As I'm heading to class, I receive another text.

Distracted, I take out my phone without checking to see who the message is from. When I read the text, I'm jerked back to reality in an instant.

Unknown: Did you enjoy realizing your mom didn't want you enough to even put her name on the birth certificate? If you think that's bad, just you wait. I've got more waiting for you. A lot more.

CHAPTER NINE

I SPEND THE REST OF THE DAY STRESSING OVER THE message until the second I walk into my house. Then my worry over the text flies right out of the window.

My dad is sitting at the kitchen table, drinking coffee and talking to Lynn about something while he reads over a piece of paper.

"Dad, you're home," I breathe in relief, wanting to get on my knees and kiss the ground.

Yes! I no longer have to do chores for Lynn and Hannah.

When he looks at me, though, my elation fizzles like flat soda.

"We need to have a talk."

"What do you mean by *we*?" I ask. "You and me, or ...?" I glance at Lynn.

She twists in her chair and smiles sweetly. "Your

father, me, and you are all going to talk." She pulls out a chair and pats the seat.

I hesitantly walk over to the table, dropping my bag on the floor before I take a seat in the chair farthest away from Lynn.

Her eyelids lower to slits, but she collects herself and reaches for the sugar dish in the middle of the table. "Your father and I are very worried about you, Isa." She scoops up a spoonful of sugar and adds it to her coffee. "Ever since you went on that trip, you've been acting like a completely different person."

"You wanted me to go on that trip," I calmly remind her.

A shrill laugh escapes her lips. "I never agreed that you could go on that trip. I was under the impression that you were going to spend the summer at your grand-mother's, getting a job and working so we would no longer have to spend so much money on you."

My fingers curl inward as I ball my hands into fists. "I pay for most of my stuff." Which is the truth. Most of my pencils, sketchbooks, and clothes have come from money I've made doing part-time jobs here and there and from the cash my grandpa gave me.

"Stop lying." She stirs her coffee, sitting in the chair with perfect posture, trying to appear like the calm, picture-perfect woman she's not. "You've been doing too much of that lately."

"I haven't lied about anything," I say, fighting to keep my temper under control.

She wipes the spoon clean on the brim of the cup before setting it down on the table. "Maybe lying isn't the right word. But you've been keeping secrets from us."

I sort through my thoughts, trying to figure out which secret she's referring to.

"I'm talking about all the snooping you've been doing," she says. "For the last couple of weeks, you've torn this house apart every time your father and I aren't around."

I glance at the paper my dad was looking at when I walked in. It looks like a receipt from a hotel in Virginia, which doesn't make any sense since he was supposed to be in Florida.

"How do you know I was looking for something?"

My dad must notice I'm looking because he folds up the paper and stuffs it into his briefcase.

"I have my ways of finding out what you've been up to." Lynn's icy gaze warns me a storm is coming for me, and I'm not going to be able to get out of its path. "That doesn't really matter. All that matters is that you found what you were looking for."

"I didn't find it." I feel like I'm walking into a trap. "I'm pretty sure Hannah left it on my bed, but I think you already know that, don't you?"

"Isabella, stop lying!" My dad suddenly explodes, slamming his fist onto the table.

I jump, my heart slamming against my chest. "Dad, I—"

"Don't you dare make excuses!" he cuts me off, stabbing a trembling finger in my direction. "You had no right to look for your birth certificate. No right at all."

"I do, too, have a right." I suck back the tears, refusing to cry in front of them. "It's *my* birth certificate. And when I turn eighteen in a few months, you would have had to give it to me anyway."

His face reddens with anger. "You don't even know what you're getting into. Just because you found out about *her*"—he flinches, casting a panicked glance in Lynn's direction—"you think you understand everything."

"What I understand is that I was lied to for years. That the people I always thought were my family weren't. That this place"—I flail my hand around at the kitchen —"wasn't always my home. That all these damn years I spent here, feeling like a fucking outcast, could've been avoided if you would've just let Grandma raise me, instead of bringing me into a family who hates me!" I'm breathing ravenously by the time I'm finished. It feels so good to get it out.

The vein in my dad's forehead bulges as he slides his hand across the table and clutches mine. "You will never talk to me that way again. Do you understand? I won't let you turn into your mother. I won't let you turn into that vile woman who ruined my life."

His fingers dig so violently into my hand I'm pretty sure I'm going to have bruises. "From now on, you will do everything Lynn and I tell you." He lets me go and pushes back from the table. "And as far as I'm concerned, *she* is your mother." He looks at Lynn before storming out of the kitchen.

"What did you think was going to happen?" Lynn says as I work to get oxygen into my lungs. "That he was going to tell you he was sorry and that deep down he really loved your mother?"

She rolls her eyes at me when I say nothing.

"Your mother was a terrible person who did terrible things to people, and we've been trying to make it so you didn't end up like her." She scoots back from the table, looking at me with hatred as she grabs my hand and pulls me to my feet. "But from what I can see, you're going to end up just like her—rotting in a grave that no one visits." She drags me with her as she heads for the doorway. "Now, you're going to come with me and paint over that god-awful painting you put up on that wall."

I can barely breathe. Barely think. Barely make sense of what she says.

My mom was a bad person?

She did terrible things?

I'm going to end up just like her?

She's dead?

I have to get out of here.

"No!" I shout, wrenching my hand from her hold. "I'm

not going to paint that fucking wall. It's *my* wall. And I like the painting."

She doesn't seem shocked by my outburst. If anything, she seems pleased, like she's gotten everything she's wanted.

"Just like your mother," she says.

I shove her, not enough to do much, but it still shocks her. Then, before she can say anything, I run out of the kitchen and out the back door.

Outside, I find Hannah getting out of her car. The sight of her makes me just about lose it.

"You did this, didn't you!" I shout as I head down the driveway toward her. "You left the birth certificate on my bed, and then told them I was looking for it. You set me up so they'd think I was the one who found it!" The closer I get to her, the angrier I get and the more words keep spilling from my lips. "And you've been sending me those texts. To mess with my head."

She looks at me like I'm the lunatic as she opens the trunk of her car and grabs some shopping bags. "Look, I don't know what your deal is, but I've never texted you." She closes the trunk of her car then turns toward me. "I don't even have your phone number programmed into my phone."

"You're such a liar," I say through gritted teeth.

"No, I'm not." Her lips twist into a grin. "Trust me; if I did set you up for something, I'd be bragging about it."

With that, she walks up the driveway and disappears into the house, leaving me to stew in my confusion.

What if she's telling the truth? What if it wasn't her? Then who else could it be? Lynn? Quite possibly. And what about what Indigo said about my dad being behind all the text messages? Why would he do that, though? Does he hate me that much?

The truth crashes down on me. Yes, I think he really might hate me that much.

Tears start to spill from my eyes as I race down the sidewalk, trying to figure out what to do next. I think about running to town or texting Grandma Stephy or Indigo to come get me, but before I can get that far, Kai appears at the corner of the sidewalk.

He starts to turn away the moment he spots me then notices the tears in my eyes and rushes toward me. "What's wrong?"

I shake my head. "I can't ..." I suck in a huge breath of air. "I can't ..." I start to sob hysterically and my legs buckle. "My mom's dead."

Kai catches me before I hit the ground and pulls me against his chest. I pull back, feeling moronic for having a meltdown in front of him, but he only presses me closer and lets me cry into his shirt.

"It's going to be okay," he says, smoothing his hand up and down my back. "I promise."

I wish he was right. I wish this was all a bad dream or something that I could eventually get over. Maybe one day I will. Maybe one day it won't hurt so badly. Right now, the pain is suffocating way more than the shell I used to live in, and I'm unsure how to make it go away or if it'll ever go away completely.

So I do the only thing I can do for now. I cry as hard as I can, letting it all out, grateful Kai is there to keep me from falling down completely.

CHAPTER 10
KAI

I DON'T KNOW WHAT TO DO TO HELP HER. ALL I KNOW IS that I wish I could take her pain away.

I've always had a soft spot for Isa, ever since seventh grade, way before her girlie makeover. To be honest, I think I might be in love with her, but that's a confession I'll never say aloud. It doesn't really matter anyway. I messed our friendship up by being a pussy and not standing up to my friends. I'm not like that anymore, though, haven't been for a while.

Over the last year, I tried to become friends with Isa again, but every time I opened my mouth, she got pissed off. She's the only girl that's ever called me out on my bullshit, who's cared enough about me to ask if I'm okay, and one of the few girls who hasn't tried to use me to get to Kyler.

It pisses me off that he's trying to date her now. He

didn't even give her the time of day until a few weeks ago. He still has no clue what makes Isa so amazingly different from everyone else.

God, what I'd give to kiss her again. Only this time, we'd both be sober. I almost did it while we were in the tree, but I chickened out because I saw her hesitate. I know what that hesitation means. It means she didn't want to kiss me. More than likely, she was thinking of Kyler.

Fucking story of my life.

"Kai, I think my mom's dead," Isa whispers. She's repeated that a few times now.

Her face is still pressed to my chest, which hurts like a bitch. I'm pretty sure T broke a rib when he punched me earlier today. The punch was just the start of things if I can't come up with the money I owe him. Or that Bradon owes him, anyway.

Somehow, I got caught up in this fucking mess after stupidly vouching for Bradon, even though I knew I shouldn't. And now I'm the one T's coming after.

"Why do you think she's dead?" I rub up and down Isa's back. My touch seems to soothe her.

"Lynn just told me she was." Her voice is hoarse. "She said she was a bad person, and that she is rotting in her grave now."

I shake my head. Fucking Lynn. That woman is a bitch, just like her mini-me clone of a daughter.

"Isa, you know Lynn could be lying to you, right? She's not a reliable source."

"Yeah, I know." She sniffles into my shirt. "But what if she's not lying? What if she's telling the truth?"

I think about the papers I tucked away in my back pocket about an hour ago, the papers Big Doug gave me from all the information he dug up on Isa's mom.

"But she might not be." I want to tell her what I know, but I'm worried she'll completely break apart if I do it right now.

Isa's a strong girl. She's had to be with all the shit she's put up with at home. But this is big. If I wait a few days, she'll be able to handle the news better, and that might give me enough time to get some more information on why her mom's in jail in Virginia.

The papers say it's for murder charges, though there's not a lot of details. I'm not buying the story yet. If there's one thing I've learned over the last couple of months, it's never assume things are what they appear to be.

"Why do your stomach muscles keep tightening?" she asks, pulling back to look at me. Her eyes are swollen, and she's got the whole raccoon look going on. She still looks beautiful, though. "Am I hugging you too hard?"

I snort a laugh. "Yeah, your tiny, little arms are giving me boo-boos."

That gets her to smile. Then she instantly frowns as her eyes well up again.

"Hey, I have an idea." I drape my arm over her shoulders and steer her toward my house. "How about we go inside, get you some chocolate, and watch *Zombieland*?" I know she won't refuse. Sugar and zombies are the keys to her heart.

"Thanks, Kai. You're such a good friend," she says, wiping her eyes with her sleeves. "Seriously, I don't know what I'd do without you."

My lip twitches at the "friend" reference. I remind myself that it's for the best, at least until I get this shit with T sorted out. The last thing I want to do is drag her into that mess. After that, though, all bets are off. That kiss in the tree will happen … when she's ready.

She may think she likes Kyler, that he's the one for her, but she's wrong. Kyler doesn't get her like I do. He doesn't know how to make her laugh, doesn't know how to talk comic book and superhero crazy talk with her like I do.

I just hope one day she realizes that.

ABOUT THE AUTHOR

Jessica Sorensen is a *New York Times* and *USA Today* best-selling author who lives in the snowy mountains of Wyoming. When she's not writing, she spends her time reading and hanging out with her family.

Secrets & the Spies

Confessions & a Secret (coming soon)

My Life with the Band

Discovering Benton

Whispered Secrets & a Kiss

Untitled (coming soon)

The Illusion Series:

The Illusion of Annabella

The Mysteries of Star Grove

Suspicion

Untitled (coming soon)

Rules of Willow & Beck:

Rules of Willow & Beck

Untitled (coming soon)

The Confession of Luna:

The Confessions of Luna

Untitled (coming soon)

Secrets Never Die:

Secrets Never Die

Untitled (coming soon)

Lexi Ashford Series:

The Diary of Lexi Ashford

The Diary of Lexi Ashford: The Agreement

Untitled (coming soon)

The Heartbreaker Society:

The Opposite of Ordinary

The Simplicity in Ordinary

Untitled (coming soon)

The Unraveling Mysteries Series:

The Mysterious Guy Next Door

The Mystery of the Symbol

The Forgotten Memory

The Suspicious Note

Untitled (coming soon)

A Pact Between the Forgotten:

The Art of Being Friends

The Rules of Being Friends

The Art of Kissing (coming soon)

Shadow Cove Series:

Spies & Sprinkles

Secrets & Vanilla Bean Frosting (coming soon)

The Coincidence Series:

The Coincidence of Callie and Kayden

The Redemption of Callie and Kayden

The Destiny of Violet and Luke

The Truth of Violet and Luke

The Promise of Violet and Luke

The Evermore of Callie and Kayden

Seth & Greyson

The Coincidence Mysteries:

Callie & the Start of a Mystery

Untitled (coming soon)

The Secret Series:

The Prelude of Ella and Micha

The Secret of Ella and Micha

The Forever of Ella and Micha

The Temptation of Lila and Ethan

The Ever After of Ella and Micha

Lila and Ethan: Forever and Always

Ella and Micha: Infinitely and Always

The Secret Star Grove Mysteries:

Ella & the Interrupted Road Trip

Ella & the Welcome Home

Untitled (coming soon)

Breaking Nova Series:

Breaking Nova

Saving Quinton

Delilah: The Making of Red

Nova and Quinton: No Regrets

Tristan: Finding Hope

Wreck Me

Ruin me

Unbeautiful Series:

Unbeautiful

Untamed

Tangled Realms:

Forever Violet

Untitled (coming soon)

Harlynn's Mystery Investigations:

Sugar Cookies & Zombie Secrets

Untitled (coming soon)

Mystic Willow Bay Vampires

Tempting Raven

Enchanting Raven

Alluring Raven

Untitled (coming soon)

Mystic Willow Bay Mysteries Series:

The Secret Life of a Witch

Broken Magic

Stolen Kisses

One Wild, Crazy, Zombie Night

Magical Whispers & the Undead

Untitled (coming soon)

Enchanted Chaos Series:

Enchanted Chaos

Shimmering Chaos

Iridescent Chaos (coming soon)

Capturing Magic:

The Thief of Wishes

The Thief of Magic

Untitled (coming soon)

My Cursed Superhero Life:

Grim

Untitled (coming soon)

Guardian Academy Series:

Entranced

Entangled

Enchanted

Entice

Charmed

Untitled (coming soon)

Monster Academy for the Magical:

Monster Academy for the Magical

Monster Academy for the Magical: Hidden Magic

Monster Academy for the Magical: The Monster Trial

Untitled (coming soon)

The Shattered Promises Series:

Shattered Promises

Fractured Souls

Unbroken

Broken Visions

Scattered Ashes

The Fallen Star Series:

The Fallen Star

The Underworld

The Vision

The Promise

The Lost Soul

The Evanescence

The Mist of Stars (untitled)

The Darkness Falls Series:

Darkness Falls

Darkness Breaks

Darkness Fades

The Death Collectors Series (NA and YA):

Ember X and Ember

Cinder X and Cinder

Spark X and Spark

Standalones:

The Forgotten Girl